THE LAST FANG OF GOD

RYAN KIRK

WATERSTONE
MEDIA

For Chester

A BITTER WIND

Kalen woke with a start as the shadow crossed the doorway to his bedroom. His right hand went to the sheathed dagger under his pillow while his left shielded his eyes from the dying light of the fire in the main room.

The figure slumped against the doorframe as though exhausted from running a race. Kalen's eyes adjusted to the light, and he saw it was Sascha. Her nightgown was damp and clung to her body. Long brown hair fell over her shoulders and halfway down her back. It had escaped from its braid and hung loose, wet with sweat.

"Sascha?" He released the dagger and sat up.

He noticed her eyes, then. They were wide, and though her pupils were pointed at him, they didn't see him. She looked beyond him, wandering the realm of gods. His heart broke at the sight, and the world tilted beneath him, dumping him out of his warm and comfortable home and into dark uncertainty.

He'd seen the signs before but, like a fool, had ignored them.

Life returned to her gaze, and she focused on him. She frowned and looked around as though uncertain why she stood at his doorway. Then she coughed up blood. More blood trickled from the corner of her mouth and dribbled down her chin, then dripped onto her nightgown.

Sascha looked down at the stain, then brought her fingers to her lips. They came away red.

She looked up, worry on her face. "Dad?"

Then, before he could react, her eyes rolled up, and she pitched forward. Kalen leaped from the bed with a speed any of the young men in the village would envy and caught his daughter before she struck the ground. He grunted as her weight surprised him. It had been years since she'd let him pick her up, and she'd grown into a strong young woman in that time.

He turned her over in his arms and wiped her chin with his sleeve. He pressed his hand against the center of her chest. Her heartbeat was strong, and he breathed a slow sigh of relief. He gently pulled apart her eyelids. Her dark brown eyes weren't dilated, but the light that animated them was gone.

Kalen told himself the light would return in time. He supported her back with his left arm and worked his right underneath her knees. Then he picked her up, carrying her like he had when she was little and the future was bright.

Traces of the girl she'd been remained, especially as she slept. When she was at peace, it was easy to remember the happy child she'd once been. It was easier to remember the warmth and love she'd spread wherever she roamed.

Kalen stood and took a moment to make sure he was balanced before he took her back to her bedroom. He turned sideways through the door, careful not to bump her against the frame.

Sascha's room looked like a storm had passed through. Blankets were strewn everywhere. Kalen placed his daughter gently in her bed, noting that it, too, was damp with sweat. Then he gathered the blankets up and covered her. He put the back of his hand against her forehead.

She was burning.

He stood and watched her for a time. Her breaths were even, and though she tossed and turned, the worst of the attack seemed to be over. Still, he watched for a while longer, leaning against a wall.

He sniffed, and his sharp nose caught another scent. Someone else had been in this room not all that long ago. Probably Rolf, Kalen figured. The boy's muscles had outgrown his intelligence about ten years ago, but he was the strongest of the young men in the village by far and had a winning smile.

Kalen wanted to tell Sascha to wait for someone better. He wanted to tell her the world was so much wider than she understood.

Not that she would listen.

He wouldn't have at that age, either.

When he was sure the worst had passed, he left the bedroom and closed the door behind him. He put another log on the fire, then returned to his room and threw on a clean tunic and pants.

Kalen stopped by Sascha's door before he left. She didn't stir.

He didn't want to leave, but he had to be certain. If tonight were what he expected, she'd be in no further danger while she slept. It was a warning and no more. He threw on a cloak and left the warmth of his house.

The night was cool but not unpleasant. In a previous life, it would have been the sort of night Kalen would have watched the stars with his pack, howling at the moon as it rose. They might have hunted, trusting the ever-watchful eyes of Vilkas to protect them from the dangers the darkness held.

There was no such excitement here. In this village, the young didn't even keep watch. Homes were quiet, their residents asleep. The wisps of smoke that rose from the chimneys were the only sign of life. Kalen turned left, passed half a dozen houses, then stopped at a door near the other side of the settlement.

He raised his hand to knock, but a voice welcomed him from within. "Come in, Kalen."

He grunted and opened the door.

Sonje's home was less than half the size of his own, but the fire blazed. He started to sweat, so pulled off his cloak. "You knew I was coming."

Sonje had seen far more years than Rolf could count to, and even Kalen didn't dare guess her age. Despite her advanced years, she moved with the strength and grace of a woman half as old. Her hair, white as a fresh coating of snow under the full moon, was pulled back in a tight bun. Her wrinkles were deeper than some canyons Kalen had navigated, but her eyes twinkled in the firelight, and when he visited, she always had the corner of her lip turned up in a smile as though privy to some joke no one else could hear.

Sonje shrugged. "Didn't cast about you, but sometimes you get stuck in my readings, anyway. Annoying habit of yours, honestly. This morning I was casting for Solina. She wanted to know where to graze her sheep, and instead, I find out you'll be visiting me tonight after all decent folk have gone to bed."

Kalen arched an eyebrow. "You were casting for *grazing advice*?"

She swatted away his question like an obnoxious fly. "Of course I wasn't. What I was casting for is between Solina, Bonde, and me."

"So you know why I'm here?"

"No. I only knew that you would visit tonight." She was sitting cross-legged on the floor, and she gestured for him to join her. "So, what merits such a late-night visit?"

"I'd like you to cast for Sascha."

Sonje's eyes narrowed. "Why me? You could cast for her with far more ease."

He bowed his head to the floor. "Where Sascha is involved, my will is as clear as mud, and that's doubly true tonight. You're the only one I'd trust with a rune."

Sonje's reply was long in coming. "Could you be more specific? I've avoided the blood of Vilkas for good reason."

"I know. She woke me up earlier, her gaze distant. I believe she was spirit walking. When she woke, she coughed up blood and didn't know where she was."

"Rise, Kalen. I won't have you groveling before me."

Kalen rose, but the hard look on Sonje's face didn't reassure him.

"If it is as you say, you know as well as I what that means. Why ask me to cast for you?" she asked.

"I would know Bonde's tale. You told us, at her birth, she would be protected."

Sonje bit her lower lip. "You still treat the gods with contempt."

Kalen didn't deny it. "Sonje, please. I must know."

"Fine. You have her blood?"

Kalen unrolled the shirt he'd used to wipe Sascha's blood from her chin. Sonje reached behind her and grabbed a leather bag. The polished stones within clacked together. She reached in, took out one rune, then held out her other hand to Kalen. He handed her the shirt, and she wiped his daughter's blood on the stone. Then she returned the shirt to him.

What followed was a familiar ritual, though Kalen had rarely seen Sonje perform her craft. She took out a square of linen, slightly larger than a handkerchief, with small runes stitched around the border. She spread it flat on the floor, smoothing out the creases with the back of her hand.

Then she reached back into her bag and grabbed eight more runes. They joined the first, and Sonje held them in her cupped hands. She whispered, her voice so quiet not even Kalen could hear.

He sensed the power in the words, though. The air hummed as though vibrating to her voice. The power pressed against him, and he winced as though someone was screaming in his ears.

Sonje turned pale and stopped whispering. The air within the home calmed. She glanced up at Kalen, begging him with her eyes not to ask her again.

He understood, but it was for Sascha. "Please."

She nodded, looking like a prisoner of war being led to their execution. "Perhaps it is best if you step outside. I do not trust Bonde's runes in your presence."

That was probably wise. Kalen uncrossed his legs and stood. "I'll be right outside. Thank you."

He didn't bother with his cloak. Sonje's home was so

warm that he was sweating almost as much as his daughter had been earlier. He embraced the cool night air and stared up at the moon. Tonight, the familiar sight provided him no relief.

He couldn't hear Sonje anymore, but he felt the power of her runes, even though he stood outside her home. The power was greatly lessened, though, and he didn't fear for the ancient seer.

Her strength waned as she read the runes. Kalen waited, fighting the temptation to barge back in and attempt to interpret her runes for himself. He'd already been gone from Sascha for too long.

In due time, Sonje called him back. The sweat had cooled from his face and arms, and the warmth of her home comforted him. When he entered, she was wiping Sascha's blood off the rune. She gestured for him to sit.

She didn't make him ask. "It is as you suspect. The blood of the wolf runs too strong, and the tree calls her."

"Shit."

"Indeed. I'm sorry to be the bearer of such cruel news. It puts you both in a precarious situation."

"That's putting it mildly," he said, failing to keep the bitterness from his voice. "What happened to her protection?"

"Bonde fought as well as he was able, but he was overpowered."

"By Vilkas? He's as good as dead."

"You know as well as anyone there's no creature more dangerous than the one close to death with nothing to lose. I imagine he fought tooth and nail, and Bonde has always been weak against the sword."

Kalen ran his hand through his short hair. "How long does she have?"

"You would know better than I. All Bonde says is that if the girl isn't offered to Vilkas by the turning of the year, she will die. But if her will isn't strong enough, it may not be even that long."

Kalen unconsciously brought his hand to his throat. His thoughts ran along dark paths. "That's not long, either way."

"I know. I'm sorry, Kalen."

He sat there, unmoving. He almost hesitated to ask the question. "What if we didn't leave? What if a few months here is better for her than the alternative?"

He appreciated that Sonje didn't reject the question out of hand. As a runemaster, she understood well enough. "I couldn't say. But if that was your decision, I'd be obligated to inform Lysabel, and I doubt she'd allow you to stay. Not if Sascha's been called by Vilkas."

When he still didn't move, Sonje tried another approach. "If you want, I could tell Lysabel anyway. She would probably banish you both, but it would take the weight of the decision off your shoulders."

Kalen was tempted, but he shook his head. "I appreciate the offer, but Sascha deserves the full truth. And, if the gods have any kindness left in their decaying bones, she'll have a chance to return here. I can't take that from her."

Sonje gave him a brief bow. "Good luck."

Kalen stood again and threw his cloak over his shoulders. "Thank you. When it comes to Sascha, I think I'll need it."

REFUSAL

Sascha woke with a headache that felt like someone had taken an axe to her skull. She groaned, rolled over on her side, and clutched at her head.

Her dad called from the other side of the bedroom door. "Is anything wrong?"

Even through the door and her splitting headache, she heard the concern in his voice.

Everything was wrong. She never woke up feeling like this, and from the light coming through the window, she'd slept in, too. Which meant Dad shouldn't be home, either. He always rose before the sun and was gone soon after. Not only that, but her bed felt damp.

She cast off her covers. "No, I'm fine. Just a bit of a headache."

When she sat up, she saw the blood on her nightgown. She rolled her tongue around in her mouth and tasted the metallic tang on her lips. How had it dripped from her mouth to her nightgown while she was sleeping?

Everything came back to her like a nightmare. She'd

been running for endless miles, pursued by ravens, bears, and owls. But none so fierce as the scorpion, which had pursued her long after the others had given up the chase.

It wasn't just the pursuit that inspired her to run. She'd been afraid of what chased her, yes, but something even more terrifying had pulled her forward, hauling her in with the strength of a dozen men. Then she'd seen a tree, and she'd woken in her dad's room, his eyes wide with fear.

She stood up, her knees shaky. She gingerly peeled off her night robe and dressed. When she opened the door to the rest of their house, she saw her dad fussing over a bowl of porridge.

"Now I know something's wrong," she said.

Though his back was turned, she could feel the tension radiating from him. He turned to her, a bowl of porridge in each hand and a forced smile on his face. "I made breakfast."

"So I see. What happened last night?"

He set the bowls down, then scurried over to grab spoons. He poured water from a pitcher into two mugs. She glared at him. He was delaying, and she didn't have time for this. "Dad! What happened last night?"

He sighed as he sat down. His hair looked grayer than before, as though he'd aged overnight. "Last night, you woke me up. I believe you were spirit walking. You were sweating and bleeding. After waking me, you collapsed in my room. I carried you to your bed and tucked you in. Come, sit down."

Sascha decided she'd rather stand. Dad was a terrible liar, and there was more he wasn't telling her. She crossed her arms and glared. Usually, that was more than enough to break him.

He gestured at her bowl, his eyes locked on the table.

"Please come sit down. We need to talk, and your porridge is getting cold."

"It tastes better that way, anyway. What aren't you telling me?" She didn't mean to snap at him, but he was frustrating her the same way he always did. He was treating her like she was a little girl, unable to handle adult concerns. He couldn't see that she had grown up before his eyes. By the gods, some days she was more the adult than he was.

His face hardened, but he kept his temper under control. He took several breaths through his nose. When his breathing had evened out, he tried again. "I'd really like it if you'd sit down and we can eat. We have some big decisions we have to make together."

She didn't budge. Whenever he talked about "making decisions together," what he really meant was that he'd decided already, and he'd keep explaining why until she agreed. He rarely convinced her, but agreeing was the only way to end the suffering. "What decision?"

Once again, Dad visibly mastered himself. His hands were in tight fists on top of the table, and he opened them and relaxed them. He pressed his palms into the table and exhaled sharply. "We need to leave the village."

Sascha stared at him in silence. She understood the words, but they made no sense. Finally, she snorted out a derisive laugh. "You're joking."

She'd lived in this village her entire life. And now he wanted to leave because she had one awful night of sleep? Without even discussing it?

Her rage burned hot enough that she imagined she could reheat her porridge just by holding the bowl in her hands.

"I'm not joking, girl."

She grimaced. She hated when he called her girl. Everyone else could see she was close to marrying age. Why couldn't he?

He'd stopped, not because he'd noticed her reaction, but because, once again, he was hiding something from her.

"I'm not leaving," she said, stomping her foot for good measure. "If you want to go someplace else, I won't stop you. But I'm staying right here."

His brow furrowed, and she recognized his temper was about to get the better of him. Her head still hurt, every beat of her heart causing a fresh wave of agony to wash across her eyes. "I'm sorry, Dad. I can't do this today." She strode toward the door but didn't escape before Dad's temper broke.

"You'll stay right here!"

She hurried out the door and slammed it behind her. She looked left and right, glad everyone else was already in the fields. The late summer morning sun warmed her skin, and her headache faded a little. She walked quickly away from their home while listening for the sound of the door. Dad didn't like making a scene in front of the neighbors, but he'd been angry enough he might not care.

By the time she'd turned the corner of a neighbor's house and put her own out of sight, she was confident he wouldn't follow. Dad's temper was a fierce beast, a monster always lurking beneath the surface. Even she had to acknowledge he controlled it well, though. She knew others who let anger overwhelm them, who struck others or threatened them.

Dad wasn't like that. He might shout loud enough to shake the walls, and he'd crushed his fair share of cups in his mighty hands, but Sascha had never once feared he would strike her.

That didn't mean his anger didn't frighten her, though. When it gripped him, his eyes turned cold and hard, and the warmth and passion she usually associated with him died.

She left the village, walking along a well-worn footpath that led west toward a grove of trees. Rolf liked to hide in the grove when he wasn't feeling like working, and she craved the feeling of his brawny arms.

When she reached the grove, though, he wasn't there. She wasn't that surprised. Some farmers already had crops for harvesting, and there was much work to be done. She was disappointed, though. She could have convinced Rolf to massage her scalp and banish the last of the lingering headache.

Sascha found a spot beside a tree in the sun. She sat, her back against the gnarled bark, and closed her eyes. Above, a pair of bluebirds sang to one another. The pain in her head faded like the darkness of night giving way to morning. That, combined with the distance from Dad, allowed her to think clearly for the first time today. He'd been serious about leaving.

Why? What wasn't he telling her?

He'd said that she'd been spirit walking. In the middle of the argument, the claim had barely registered, but now she focused on that. How could *she* spirit walk? The only one in the village capable was Sonje, and even she claimed it was a rare occurrence. It couldn't be true. She'd just had a nightmare and walked in her sleep. That had worried Dad, and he overreacted. He did that often when she was involved. He was so scared of losing her the way he'd lost Mom, he couldn't think straight. She'd let his temper cool. Then they could talk tonight.

She tried to imagine leaving and couldn't. She talked

about traveling often enough, usually with Rolf. But with Rolf, it was sharing a daydream. He'd never leave this place, no matter how often he claimed this village was too small for his ambitions. Rolf didn't speak like Dad, whose every word reverberated with intent. When Dad said they were leaving, their departure became something real and immediate, and she found she wasn't ready. They had it good here. When she thought about leaving everything behind, a tear came unbidden to her eye.

"Now, now. There's nothing a beautiful young woman like you should cry about on a morning like this."

Sascha nearly jumped out of her skin. She could have sworn she was alone in the grove. She snapped her head around and saw an old man leaning against another tree. Shadows fell over him like a cloak, but his teeth shone white when he smiled.

He was hard to look at. Not in the sense that he was hideous or deformed, but because her eyes wanted to slide off him. The harder she focused, the more indistinct he became. She rubbed her eyes with the palms of her hands. That headache had been the worst she'd ever had, and apparently, she still wasn't fully recovered.

She could tell he was old, though. Maybe more than old. His arms were nearly as thin as a sapling's branches and as pale as the moon. His voice was soft, but she sensed something behind it that she couldn't describe. Not a power, exactly, but an authority, perhaps. An intent, like every word mattered.

Like her father.

He flashed that smile, which seemed too bright for the shadows. "Sorry to startle you."

Sascha found her manners. "No, I should be the one apologizing. I didn't realize there was anyone else here."

"It's no problem. I've been here a long time and appreciate the company."

She frowned at that, only now realizing she didn't recognize the stranger. He wasn't from the village or any of the surrounding areas. She should leave and tell someone about the outsider, but she felt no sense of danger from him. Given how weak he looked, she could easily run away if he attacked. So she stayed where she was. "Who are you? A traveler?"

She couldn't imagine him traveling far but didn't want to assume.

"Of a sort, though not by choice. I'm originally from much farther north. Who are you?"

"Sascha. I live in the village down the path."

"It's a pleasure to meet you for the first time, Sascha. If you don't mind me asking, why the tears? Did young Rolf hurt your feelings?"

"No. It's my dad. He's saying we need to leave, and I'm realizing that I don't want to. I want to stay here," she said.

The older man stroked his chin. "Your dad, you say? It's no wonder you're upset."

"You know him?"

"Oh, your father and I go back a long way. He's a frustrating man," he said.

Finally, someone who understood. "What do you think I should do?" she asked.

"Kalen is a troublesome man to reason with. It's part of what makes him dangerous. When his will is focused, even the gods tremble at what he's capable of."

Sascha scoffed. "Dad? Dangerous? He's an excellent shot with a bow, but he's hardly dangerous."

The eyes of the stranger turned to her and stared through her. "You don't know, do you?"

"Know what?" she asked.

The stranger's smile flashed again, and Sascha turned away. It was easier to look anywhere else. "You're like him, aren't you? Too much will and not enough wisdom. Let me show you the way I used to show him," he said.

Sascha's stomach felt unsettled. The hairs on her neck prickled. For the first time since this conversation had started, she recognized that something felt wrong. When she tried to decide what, her thoughts became cloudy. "What will you show me?"

"You should go now," the stranger said.

Sascha stood obediently. "Where should I go?"

"Back home. Your father is gone; off to prepare for your departure. Underneath your table, there is a loose floorboard. Pry it up, and discover for yourself the truths your father never saw fit to share with you."

Sascha left the small grove. As she did, the last of her headache vanished, but with the headache went her memories. She'd spoken with someone in the grove, a man who had known far too much. She couldn't remember his face, his voice, or even what they'd spoken about.

All she remembered was that there was a secret in her house under the table. A secret under the floorboards she intended to discover right away.

BARGAIN

Kalen watched Sascha as she stormed from their house and slammed the door behind her. He rose to give chase, but now that she was gone, the tightness in his chest relaxed and his thoughts came more clearly. He'd done a poor job of breaking the news to her.

This was her home, and he'd told her they were leaving with no warning. All because she hadn't wanted the porridge he'd made for her.

He slumped back in his chair, wishing he could jump back into the past and try again. Gods, half the time they spoke, he wished the same. He reached under his tunic and pulled out a pendant on a thin chain. It was engraved with the image of a tree, and he rubbed it between his thumb and forefinger.

Embla had given it to him long ago, soon after they'd met. It was to remind him of the home he'd left behind and the home he'd built with his own two hands.

His heart slowed, and he leaned back and stared at the ceiling. He imagined Embla standing behind him, strong thumbs digging into his shoulders after he'd spent a backbreaking day in the fields.

He spoke into the empty air, wishing she could break through the veil and answer. "Could really use your advice right about now."

As always, the empty house gave no answers. His runes might, but he hadn't dared cast them for years. Life was hard enough without the gods meddling in it.

He sighed and stood. Arguments or not, they'd have to leave soon, so there was much to do. He'd already excused himself from the day's labors on account of Sascha's illness, but that had only been the start.

Kalen pushed open the door, stepped into the morning sunlight, and shut it gently behind him. His first visit was to Sonje, because that conversation was the easier of the two. He knocked on her door and was greeted by a bleary-eyed and messy-haired seer.

"What do you want? It's too early for your crap," she croaked.

Kalen looked toward the east, where the sun was already high in the sky.

"Shut up," Sonje said.

Kalen grinned. "I only came to check on you. Last night must have been trying."

It was a mark of how long they'd known each other that he knew she was about to make some sort of cutting remark about *him* being trying. She reconsidered and asked the more important question. "Did you tell her?"

"I did, but not well. She's probably off pouting in the grove."

"You should have told her who you were long ago. Who she is. It's going to be much harder for her now."

Kalen nodded. "One of many pieces of your advice I didn't take that I'm sure I'll regret. Perhaps I was a fool to hope, but I wanted something better for her. I wanted this for her."

Sonje stepped out of her house and stretched in the morning sun. "It was well-intentioned but still foolish. We'll never know where to go if we don't know where we've been."

"A lesson I hope I someday learn. Is there anything I can do for you before we leave?"

Sonje shook her head. "I'll miss you, though. Lysabel won't admit it, but I'm not sure this village would have grown the way it did without you. You've done the work of three men, and your presence has kept people's more destructive impulses in check. And don't think I don't know you've gone out into the night hunting several times since you arrived."

Kalen gave the runemaster a sharp look. "Only when it was necessary."

"I'll give you another piece of advice, old friend. People don't change that much. It's true of you, too."

"Here I was, hoping you'd give me the secret of getting Sascha to listen to me."

Sonje waved the request away. "*Bah.* You two are too much alike. She's always listening, though. Trust me on that. Children always are."

It wasn't what Kalen had hoped for, but it would have to do. "Well, I appreciate everything you've done, too."

"It was nothing. And it was a pleasure to have a runemaster such as you to talk to. I like the quiet of this village, but people here don't follow the old ways like they should."

Kalen looked around to make sure they were

unobserved, then dropped into a deep bow—the same he would have given his chief once.

Sonje knew what it meant. When he rose, her eyes were watering. "I won't offer you the blessing of the gods, but I will wish you well, old friend."

"Take care, Sonje."

He turned and swallowed the lump in his throat. Now he regretted not saving that parting for last.

He found Lysabel helping a group of farmers with the harvest. She glared when she saw him, wiping some of the sweat from her brow. She was older than him, her blonde hair slowly turning gray.

"Can we speak in private?" he asked.

She looked at the field; the work for the day barely started. Her expression told him she'd rather be doing anything else, but when he didn't back down, she relented. She put down her tools and told the others she'd return shortly, putting a strong emphasis on how quickly she'd be returning.

"What is it?" she asked.

"Sascha and I will leave soon. Either today or tomorrow."

"How long will you be gone?"

"Not sure. Could very well be forever."

That got her attention. "Why?"

"A personal matter."

She frowned. Lysabel knew enough of his past to be wary of personal matters, but she didn't understand him like Sonje did. She'd been ordered to let him settle in the village, orders written by the chief himself. It still grated on her more than a decade later.

When she didn't immediately respond, Kalen egged her on. "I thought you'd be overjoyed."

"Ecstatic. But my father taught me that when something seems too good to be true, it usually is. What aren't you telling me?"

"Nothing that concerns you. I wanted to let you know, out of respect for the kindness you've shown us, but I also wanted to talk about the house."

"What about it?" she asked.

If there was anything Kalen was going to miss about the village besides Sonje, it was the house. He'd built it with his own hands, aided by several of the villagers. It was the first time he'd built something, and it had rooted him here better than anything else could have.

"I'd like someone to care for it while we're gone. If neither of us is back by this time next year, you have my permission to sell it and spread the wealth around the village."

She put her hands on her hips. "Caring for it will be easy enough. Keeping it empty might not."

The village had been attracting several new arrivals. Most were warriors moving deeper into clan land after their years of service.

Kalen guessed her angle easily enough. "You can rent it, but anyone living there needs to vacate if we return."

"Deal," Lysabel said.

There was one other possibility that Kalen hadn't wanted to consider, but he'd be a fool not to make plans for it. "There's one other thing."

"What?"

Kalen thought of the journey ahead of them, the dangers both known and unknown. "There's a chance that Sascha may return without me. If that comes to pass, I want your word she'll be given the house and anything else due to me."

Lysabel's eyes narrowed. "But only within the year you specified?"

Kalen clenched his fist, but Lysabel didn't flinch. She ran the village well and was generous enough when it mattered. Over the years, the village had become her whole life. Its success was her success. If she had any weakness, it was that she sometimes thought more about the village as a whole and how it could grow instead of the people who lived within it.

He thought of Sonje's lament, that there were few here who kept the old ways. Lysabel was an example, more concerned with the letter of her promises than with the spirit of them.

He wouldn't miss bargaining with her, that much was certain. "Yes, only within the year that is specified. If she hasn't returned by then, I don't think she will."

Lysabel tapped her foot and stared hard at him. Kalen supposed such a glare might intimidate others, but he found Lysabel's antics more amusing than threatening. She thought she was tough, but she'd not been forged in the blood, mud, and suffering of battle.

And that wasn't all a bad thing, Kalen decided. If he'd had more of a choice, he would have preferred Sascha to have such an upbringing as well. His years here had been the most peaceful of his life, and that was good.

Finally, Lysabel agreed. "I will make sure that we care for your house for one year, starting from tomorrow."

Kalen was sure she considered the "from tomorrow" addition a sign of her incredible generosity. He let her bask in her self-satisfied glory. "Thank you."

"It would help if you told me where you were going and why."

She was prying, but Kalen didn't blame her. He'd caused her no trouble while he lived here, but his comings and goings had made her curiosity insatiable. Unfortunately for her, the nature of his oaths and the safety of his family meant she'd have to content herself with never knowing.

"Good day, Lysabel, and thank you for your kindnesses over the years. I shall let the chief know of you if I speak to him again."

He turned and left before she could ask more questions.

Still, she asked one of his retreating back. "You're going off to war, aren't you? Just like before."

He answered, though softly enough that she wouldn't hear, "Something like that."

BRANCHING PATHS

Sascha stormed into her house like a summer gale, blowing everything in her path away. Dad had cleared the table after her departure, so she shoved it to the side of the room, tipping over two of the chairs. The other two chairs she kicked to the side of the room.

A quick glance at the floorboards revealed nothing, though she wanted to believe that if one had been obviously out of place, she would have noticed during the sixteen years she'd lived here. She ran her hand lightly across the boards, but all were flush with one another.

Something was here, a secret her father had buried long ago. She couldn't say how she knew, but she was as sure of it as she knew the sun would set in the west. She stood, grabbed a knife, and pried at the seams of the boards. The first, second, and third all seemed well-secured, but the fourth allowed her knife to slip easily underneath. She levered the board up and worked her fingers under it.

She'd expected to twist and pull at the board, but she lifted it as easily as the lid on her mother's old keepsake box.

Something long was wrapped in hides under the board. It hadn't been stashed but carefully placed. Sascha reached down and pulled it out, surprised by the weight of it. Though she hadn't yet seen it, she knew what it was, and it made no sense to her.

She untied the thin cords wrapped around the hides, then unwrapped the hides. Her hands moved slowly, even as her impatience grew. Through its wrappings, she felt the power emanating from it. Power that repulsed her even as it drew her closer. This was something sacred, set apart from the ordinary life she'd always known. She was sure of it.

When she finished unwrapping the sword, she placed it in front of her.

The power she felt didn't match its appearance. She'd half expected the weapon to glow, but its sheath was unadorned, and the hilt and guard were as plain as every other sword she'd seen warriors carrying. But she still felt as though it might burn her if she touched it.

Sascha reached out her hand and gently placed one finger on the hilt. It was warm to the touch, but it did her no harm. She wrapped her right hand around the hilt. It felt like a perfect fit.

She grabbed the sheath with her other hand and tugged on the sword. It stuck at first but slid free as she applied more force. She pulled it out a bit and froze. She'd already sensed this was no ordinary sword, but now she knew why. Runes had been etched in the steel, and they hummed with strength.

This was a sword crafted by a runemaster. She pulled it out farther, reading the runes as they emerged from the sheath. Some looked familiar, but others were completely unknown. This wasn't Bonde's weapon.

"Sheath the sword, girl."

Sascha thought she'd heard every tone of voice her father possessed, that none could scare her into blind obedience any longer. But the note of command in her father's voice rang with a hidden strength she had no choice but to obey. She slammed the sword back into the sheath and laid it down.

Once the sword was out of her hands, the power that had compelled her faded. She glared at her father and pointed at the weapon. "What is this?"

"My sword. How did you find it?"

She was about to spit out an answer when she frowned. How had she found it? She'd been so certain it was there, but why? "I went to the grove, and I think I talked with someone."

No, that didn't sound right. Her thoughts were clouded. "I don't know. I was sure something was hidden underneath the table."

She expected an angry tirade, one that would shake the walls of the house and scare any neighbors within a mile. When none came, she glanced up and saw him shaking his head. His gaze traveled from the sword to her and back to the sword, then he seemed to collapse in on himself like someone had punched him in the stomach. She didn't think she'd seen him so defeated since the day they'd buried Mom.

He walked over to the chairs she'd kicked to the side and sat on one. He pushed the other in her direction. "Can we talk?"

"Will you tell me why you have a runemaster's sword hidden in our house?"

He nodded. "Part of what you need to know, anyway." He

exhaled, long and slow. "I suppose I should start a way back. Do you mind?"

For the first time in years, she was willing to listen to her father's tales. A sword like that had a story, and she wanted it. She gestured for him to continue.

"As you know, I'm not from here."

That was obvious, though the subject didn't come up much. Dad was taller than anyone in the village, and his skin was a shade paler. The difference meant little after a summer filled with days of hard labor under the sun, but it was there all the same.

He continued. "The clan I'm from is known as the Wolves of Vilkas."

Sascha interrupted. "I've never heard of them."

"You wouldn't have. For one, they've almost entirely been destroyed. But my homelands are far to the north. There's no reason you would know of them."

"Except they're your people, and thus mine. Why haven't you told me of them before?"

Her father hesitated, and Sascha feared he was about to lie or hold something back. "Dad. I think I need to know."

That settled the debate inside him. "True words, daughter, true words. I haven't told you because, as far as I know, I'm the last true-blooded Wolf of Vilkas. I'm sure there are others like you, with diluted bloodlines, but not many. We were wiped from the face of this world for our sins. I escaped and, in so doing, hoped to put my past far behind me. When you were conceived, we chose to raise you only as a child of Bonde. Unfortunately, an oath has been broken, and the blood of Vilkas is rising in you. That is why you walked the spirit world last night and why I said we must leave this morning."

Sascha's nostrils flared at the reminder, but Dad's story had hooked her. He still hadn't told her what she most wanted to know, though. "Why do you have a sword like this?"

"Because it is mine. Our clan's best swordsmith forged the sword just for me, and I etched the runes on it."

"*You're* a runemaster?" She'd never seen him sketch a rune in her life, much less use one.

"I am, or at least, I was once. I do not practice anymore."

"Why not?"

Dad's legendary temper finally started to reappear. "Were you not listening? Because I wanted to put the past behind me."

"Why?"

"Because what I did helped bring about the end of my clan!"

He clenched his hands into fists, then shook them out and pressed the palms of his hands into his eyes. "It's a story you probably deserve to hear someday, but I'd rather not relive those memories here. What is important to know is that I was once a warrior and a runemaster for the Wolves of Vilkas. The sword is mine. I escaped the destruction of my clan and made a new life here with your mom, sheltered by Bonde's mercy. My only hope was for you to live a peaceful life, but you're being called, and there's nothing either of us can do but answer."

"What if we don't?"

"Then you'll be dead by the end of the year."

～

Sascha paced back and forth, turning so often she feared she might get dizzy. Her thoughts raced faster than her feet, creating a nervous energy that made her want to run to the next village and back. But she didn't dare go too far from Sonje's door. Her irrational fear was that if she left, the old runemaster would vanish and never return.

Sonje opened the door and squinted in the bright sunlight. "By the gods, Sascha, come in and ask your questions. Your pacing is driving me to madness!"

Sonje made no secret of her displeasure, but there was a warmth to her scolding, reminding Sascha of when Rolf's grandmother used to shout at them for eating her bread before it had even cooled. The scolding served its purpose. It pulled Sascha into Sonje's home, though she wasn't sure that being here was wise. A seer's guidance was rarely straightforward.

As always, stepping into Sonje's house felt like stepping into an oven. Sweat broke out across Sascha's arms before she'd even sat down.

Sonje broke from their little traditions and spoke first. "I've been wondering when you'd visit. Been waiting for you for most of the day."

"Did you cast runes for me?"

"Not the way you think. But I had some idea what was coming and expected I might be on the short list of people you'd want to visit."

"What do you know?"

"That your father is worried sick about you and has told you he plans to leave with you."

"Do you know why?"

Sonje sat down across from her. "Of course I do. I was the

one who cast the runes for you last night and told Kalen what he already suspected. Vilkas calls for you."

"I thought that only happened in stories."

Sonje sighed. "Easy to see why you might think that, growing up here. Bonde's a different god, more passive than most. He's content with his offerings and his lot in life. Doesn't ask much from us in exchange. He's gentle compared to Vilkas and his ilk. But the gods do call, and we can do nothing but answer."

"Dad said I would die if I didn't."

"True words. Your pain will be minor at first. Headaches, stomachaches, cramps. But by the time you regret your decision, it's already too late. You're a long way from your father's homelands. It's going to be close enough as it is."

Sascha couldn't meet Sonje's steady gaze. She looked at the walls and down at the floor between them.

Sonje's voice was gentler now. "You'd hoped to hear something else?"

Sascha nodded. "Nothing he said seems real. It feels like everything I thought I knew was a lie."

"I understand how you might feel that way. But nothing's really changed, if you think about it."

Sascha lashed out. "Nothing's changed? My dad had a powerful rune sword hidden in our house. He claims he's a runemaster and that I have to leave everything I know behind!"

Sonje wasn't like her father. She didn't push back against her claims. She accepted them, then turned them on their head. "Fair enough. But your father is still the same man you've always known. He's passionate, stubborn, and not particularly farsighted. He's blinded by his own strengths.

And he also loves you more than anything else in this world, and that hasn't changed one bit."

Sascha felt the tears forming and hated that she felt like a child. "It doesn't feel that way."

"I know. Love makes fools of us all, and your father was never too far removed from foolishness to start."

Sascha wiped a tear from her eye. "If he loves me so much, why didn't he tell me any of this earlier?"

Sonje didn't answer that immediately. She was watching Sascha. "What did he say?"

"He said he wanted to protect me. But you don't protect someone by lying to their face!"

Sonje offered Sascha one of her handkerchiefs, which Sascha accepted. "May I offer another perspective?"

Sascha nodded as she wiped her tears away and blew her nose.

"When I first met your father, he carried as much guilt on his shoulders as anyone I'd ever met. I daresay I know him better than anyone now that your mom is gone, but even I only have a sense of what horrors lie buried in his past. He's got more blood on his hands than some entire clans, and he wanted so desperately to put that behind him. If your father was a farmer, he wanted to pull everything from his field. All the roots, all the stones, no matter how deep, so he could start fresh. Especially with you. He wanted you to be free of his sins. He wanted that so badly he hid the truth from you."

Sonje handed Sascha a second handkerchief. "I can't say whether he was right or wrong. More than once, I advised him to tell you at least a little in case something like this came to pass. But he held tight to his secrets, and in his defense, it gave you sixteen years of peace and happiness, which is no small thing in this cruel world."

Sonje scared many of the people in the village. Her sharp tongue cut as well as any blade, and she took no grief from anyone. She'd never frightened Sascha and had even taught her some of the basic runes of Bonde over the years. But Sascha didn't think she'd ever heard the woman speak with as much affection for anyone as she did for her father. "You think I should go with him?"

A look of pain crossed Sonje's face. "My precious child, I would do anything in my power to prevent you from going. Even with your father by your side, what will be asked of you will be painful beyond imagining. But it's the only chance at a future you have. Today is one of those days when you must choose which path you'll take. The one where you stay here is wide and easy, but also very short. The one your father will take is twisted and difficult, and there's no telling where it may lead."

Sonje offered a sad, sympathetic smile. "You've always spoken about going on an adventure. You've always wanted to see the world. Now's your chance."

Sascha shook her head. "Not like this." She rubbed the seams of the handkerchiefs between her fingers. "What else can you tell me about Dad?"

"He's a good man, if deeply flawed, and he loves you."

"That isn't what I meant."

"I know, but it's all I feel is appropriate to say. The rest should come from him instead of me."

Sascha tried a different approach. "When I pulled my dad's sword from its sheath, there were several runes etched upon it. I didn't recognize many of them. Do you have any idea what they were?"

Sonje chuckled softly. "Never. Your father and I have compared the runes of Vilkas and Bonde a handful of times but never far beyond the commonalities they share. If he could, he would take the secrets of Vilkas's runes to the grave. Even if he showed me, I'd never attempt them. Your father's skill is far beyond my own."

"But you're the village runemaster!"

That made Sonje laugh out loud. "I'm glad you believe that's worthy of such respect, but you reveal your ignorance. I'm not as skilled as those who protect our borders, and your father is something more entirely. You'll need him if you hope to survive the journey."

Sascha's thoughts traveled in a new direction. "Will I see you again?"

Sonje sighed. "Your future is far too clouded for me to see. I hope so, but I wouldn't be surprised if the answer is no."

Sascha scooted forward and embraced Sonje. "Thank you."

"I already know the gods will be with you, so I'll just wish you good health," Sonje replied.

Sascha left Sonje's home and took in the view of the village. She'd always wanted to leave, to explore the world, thanks in no small part to the stories her father had told her as she'd been growing up. It still seemed too soon.

She couldn't deny the truth before her. Dad was a liar, but he wasn't lying about this. She didn't want to die, so the path was clear.

She returned to their house, where she found Dad slowly moving around, gathering up the necessities into a pair of packs. He kept reaching toward the pendant around his neck, a sign he was thinking about Mom.

In all her discontent and anger, she'd never stopped to consider what he might think of all this. This was as sudden and unexpected for him as it was for her. Like her, he was leaving behind almost two decades of the life he'd labored hard to build.

For her.

She swallowed hard and cleared her throat. Dad looked up at her and smiled, though there was no joy behind it. The question was in his eyes.

She nodded. "Let's go."

OATHS OF OLD

Kalen was glad the paths beyond the village were easy to follow, relatively flat, and well-protected. Compared to the journey ahead, the first handful of days was a delight. They also prepared Sascha for some of what was to come. She'd never been weak, but the burden of walking more than a dozen miles a day was new to her. He checked her feet every night despite her protests.

Truth was, he wasn't that much used to it, either. He'd worked himself to the bone at the village, always eager to repay the kindness they offered by letting him build his home among them, but it wasn't the same as the journeying and fighting he'd used to do.

Mostly Sascha impressed him. She didn't complain often, and she helped with the cooking and cleaning. She was a more silent traveling companion than he preferred, but he could hardly blame her. He'd tossed her whole life on its head, and there was much to think about.

Twice at night, he heard her crying softly, but she didn't speak of it come morning, so he didn't ask. As he so often did, he wished Embla was still with them. She'd always known how to talk to Sascha, how to get their girl to share her struggles.

With anyone else, she was too much like him, shouldering the burdens and figuring life out on her own. He saw so much of him in her, and it hurt him to think he'd given her so many of his flaws.

He'd expected and prepared for an endless barrage of questions, but Sascha didn't ask any. At times, he wondered if he was being tested, that she was waiting for him to speak without her asking.

Perhaps he was a coward, but he took the easy way out. If she would not ask, he would hold on to his past for a few more days. She'd have to know eventually, but this gave her a few more days of peace.

The start of their journey carried them through the endless fields and rolling hills Bonde's people called home. When he'd last traveled these paths, he'd been heading south with Embla, Sascha already enormous in the womb. There hadn't been as many fields back then. It had been almost all grassland, with groves of trees growing by the streams. He'd been relieved that their perilous journey was nearing an end.

Today was the opposite. For another three days, they would walk in safety, but then they'd cross out of Bonde's lands and into nearly constant peril. Instead of finally finding a new home, he was leaving it. Very possibly for the last time.

They were interrupted earlier than Kalen expected. A patrol on horseback rode from west to east. When they spotted the travelers, they angled their horses to meet them on the road. Sascha tensed as they approached, the enormous warhorses looming even larger in her imagination.

Kalen tried to comfort her. "There's nothing to fear, girl. They're only protecting the clan."

He noticed how she bristled and wondered the reason. Before he could ask, the riders were upon them, pulling their mounts to a stop. Kalen offered a brief bow of respect and was pleased to see Sascha following suit. "Bonde's blessings, warriors."

"And to you, travelers." The lead rider was a young man whose physique looked like it had been chiseled from the stone of the northern mountains. He had long blond hair that hung loose. Scars covered his arms. Kalen guessed the young man had five or six years on Sascha, and he couldn't help but notice how Sascha's eyes carefully followed every movement the rider made.

Kalen almost rolled his eyes. Before today, young Rolf had been the most impressive and courageous man she'd ever met. He knew they'd talked for days about adventuring the world, but neither had taken any steps to leave the village. Likely, they never would have. Now she stood before a veteran warrior, who'd probably seen more in his years than Rolf had dreamed of seeing in a lifetime.

The rider noticed the attention, too, and seemed eager to impress the beautiful stranger. He dismounted with a flourish and bowed too deeply to Sascha. "What brings you this far north?"

"A personal matter," Kalen said.

The rider turned to Kalen and saw the sword at his hip. It was just a glance at first, but then he stopped and stared, a frown on his face. He looked from the sword to Kalen's face. "Kalen, is that you? Is that Fang?"

"I am, and it is, but I'm afraid you have me at a loss."

A wide grin broke out on the young man's face. "You wouldn't remember me. The last time we met, I couldn't have been more than seven. I'm Angar."

That name was familiar, but it took him a moment to place it. "Angar. You mean Aryn's son? By the gods, you've grown. When you were little, you kept trying to steal Fang when I wasn't looking."

Angar laughed. "I've always loved swords, and yours was the most famous I'd ever come across. Still is, now that I think about it. But you can rest easy. I know better than to cross swords with you."

"You've grown into quite the warrior. Your mother must be proud."

"Some days. She's a chief now."

"I'm glad to hear it. Few deserve the position more."

Behind Kalen, Sascha cleared her throat loudly. Kalen turned and welcomed her into the conversation. "You'll forgive my poor manners. This is Sascha, my daughter."

Angar bowed again, again more deeply than courtesy required. "The honor is mine."

When he rose, the smile had fallen from Angar's face. "Good as it is to see you, Kalen, I need to know why you're on the road. You're less than two days from the border."

"So close?" Kalen asked.

"It's been a hard summer," Angar reported with a scowl. "The scorpions have pressed us hard."

"I'm sorry to hear that. As I mentioned, our travels are a personal matter. I was hoping to speak to a chief."

Angar's eyes narrowed. "Mother is close. Less than a day's ride away."

"Would you take us to her?"

Angar debated for a moment, then agreed. "I can carry Sascha with me, if you permit."

Kalen didn't mind. The lad would not try anything untoward with Kalen near, and Kalen had little doubt Sascha would enjoy the experience. "That's fine, if my daughter wills it. I can keep pace beside you."

Angar didn't look convinced, but one glance at Kalen's sword stifled any debates. "Very well."

Angar and Sascha climbed onto Angar's horse, and they took off. Angar kept the horses at a walk, and Kalen jogged beside them. When his muscles tired, he whispered softly enough that no one could hear.

He hadn't spoken Vilkas's runes for years, but it wasn't something a runemaster forgot. His limbs filled with fresh strength, and he kept the pace all the way to the camp. The other riders sometimes watched him from the corner of their eyes, but Sascha only glanced back once. Young Angar consumed her full attention.

They reached the camp by late afternoon. Kalen felt tired, but in a good way, like he'd put in a full day in the fields helping his neighbors. His legs ached, but not so bad he wouldn't be able to run tomorrow if needed. He'd feared how his body might handle the travel, but this test gave him hope.

Being within a camp, surrounded by warriors, made him long for home. Not the house he'd built with Embla, but the home of his youth. Not a place, but a clan, always on the move.

Angar left the care of his horse to one of the other riders and led Sascha and Kalen deeper into the camp. Kalen guessed the tents held fifty or sixty warriors at most. A respectable force, but not as many as he expected.

They stopped near the center of the tents. Bonde's warriors had left a decent clearing in the heart of their camp, suitable for gathering everyone for meals and whatever passed for evening entertainment. The clearing was currently the site of a heated discussion between a small circle of warriors. Kalen recognized Aryn in the group.

The years had been kind to her. Neither face nor hair showed any distinct sign of the almost two decades that had passed since they'd last met. Physically, she couldn't intimidate anyone. She barely came up to Kalen's chest, and her arms weren't much wider than his wrists.

Kalen wondered how many of her enemies had dismissed her and died moments later. She was a skilled runemaster, and Scythe, which hung at her hip, was a work of art. Few warriors in Bonde could match her skill back when Kalen had arrived with Embla in tow. He suspected that the number had only fallen in the intervening years.

Angar stopped them well short of the meeting. "These are her commanders. I assume they'll finish shortly."

Kalen grunted his acknowledgment but had attention only for Aryn. Her eyes had the same qualities he'd noted eighteen years ago. Her sharp gaze missed little, and Kalen knew she had already observed their arrival. But the focus of her attention was on whoever in her circle was speaking. When you spoke to Aryn, you felt like you were the center of her entire world. He saw how that attention affected her commanders, how they straightened just a bit when they addressed her.

When he'd taken the chief's measure, he let his eyes wander over the camp. The tents were precisely placed, and though the camp was busy, it wasn't chaotic. Bonde's warriors had improved considerably.

The meeting ended, and the commanders bowed to Aryn. Angar brought them to Aryn, who smiled when she saw Kalen. "It's been far too long, old friend."

She honored him with the title, and he bowed deeply in response. The request he brought was no simple matter, but her kindness gave him hope she would grant it without trouble. "Your son tells me you've ascended to chief. Congratulations." He gestured to Sascha and introduced her.

Aryn favored her with a slight bow of the head. "It's a pleasure to meet you."

The chief turned back to Kalen. "May I offer you some tea? It's been a long day."

"I'd be honored."

Aryn dismissed Angar, and Kalen didn't miss the longing glance Sascha cast at his departing figure.

Kalen and Sascha followed Aryn into her tent. Aryn set a small pot of water to boiling. While she prepared the tea, they spoke of the last two decades in broad strokes. After she poured their cups, Aryn's demeanor became serious. "It is good to see you, friend, but my heart tells me you bring me bad tidings. Why are you here?"

Kalen gestured to Sascha. "She's been called by Vilkas."

"Ah." Aryn's face fell.

Another flicker of irritation passed across Sascha's face. She contained it well, remembering her manners in this unfamiliar place, but he'd have to tell her more soon. He was a coward for not telling her more already.

Kalen nodded. "We need to leave Bonde's lands and travel north, back to my homelands."

Aryn sipped at her tea but didn't answer for a long while. Kalen searched her face for some clue about how she might respond, but she gave nothing away.

Finally, she sighed and set her cup down. "You ask a very difficult thing. You swore never to leave Bonde's lands, and you swore never to draw Fang again."

"I know. If there were another way, I'd take it. But I'm asking you to release me from my vows."

"And if I don't?" Aryn asked.

"Then, for my daughter, I'd break them."

"And suffer Bonde's wrath?"

Kalen chuckled bitterly. "He would have to get in line. Compared to some of the other gods who seek my blood, I fear him little."

He saw Sascha's eyes go wide at the blasphemy, and he wondered if this meeting wouldn't have been better between just him and Aryn. Sascha wouldn't have minded a tour of the camp guided by Angar.

"His scythe has grown sharper since you last challenged him," Aryn warned.

"I don't doubt it. It doesn't change what I have to do," Kalen said.

Aryn poured herself another cup of tea. "Do you know what you ask?"

"Not entirely. I've kept to my oath all these years and rarely go much beyond Lysabel's village. I hear little of the outside world. Angar said that the scorpions have been pushing hard to the south."

"To all four corners of the map," Aryn said. "For several years after you killed Revon, they were in disarray. Our scouts found evidence of plenty of infighting, and we assumed the people of Kunama would eventually die out or join other clans. We accepted a fair number into our own ranks. Our mistake was not making sure the job was finished. About ten years ago, one of Revon's sons declared himself chief. Two years after that, Jolon won over or destroyed all the remaining factions. Since then, they've been pushing outward, winning back the territory they lost and more."

"Can we go around?" Kalen asked.

"Do you have two years to spare?"

Kalen shook his head.

"It's not just that traveling through the lands of Kunama is dangerous, Kalen. Jolon is looking for you. He believes you're the only one who can kill him, and they have sent all the clans messages demanding your head. You've been quiet, so I wasn't worried, but now here you are, walking around with Fang like nothing has changed in twenty years."

Kalen digested the new information, but Sascha didn't take it so well. "Why does the chief of another clan want to kill my dad?"

"Because in one night, your father nearly destroyed the entire clan and killed Jolon's father, the former chief." Aryn threw out the information like it was common knowledge, which, in her defense, it probably was among the warriors.

Kalen grimaced as Sascha's mouth dropped open.

Aryn turned to Kalen. "She didn't know?"

"Tried to raise her without my past haunting her steps. It's not going so well."

Sascha stood, but at least had the decency to bow to Aryn before storming out of the tent.

Aryn arched an eyebrow. "A passionate youth. She reminds me of someone else I used to know."

"True words, but it doesn't make her any easier to parent. Angar's turned out well, it seems."

"Thank you. I'm proud of the man he's become. Though a part of my heart still breaks every time he rides to battle."

"How do you do it?" Kalen asked.

Aryn shrugged. "What choice do I have? I want to protect him, but the world is cruel, and we'll say our final farewells eventually. Whenever that day comes, it will be too soon. All I can do is prepare him as best I can, which means I can't protect him. It's difficult, though."

"I'd hoped that in the village she'd never have to experience any of this."

"Noble, but misguided. A man with a past such as yours can never be completely free of it. That goes even for what you plan. Do you still think you will step foot on Kunama land?"

"I don't see how I have a choice. If I don't reach my homeland by year's end, she'll die. I don't want to fight you, though."

Aryn poured herself the last of the tea. "If you're caught anywhere near our border, Jolon will know we were hiding you and focus his revenge on us. We only survive today because his attention is torn in all directions."

She sipped from her cup, then decided. "I'll release you from your oath in exchange for a new one. If you're going to tread among the scorpions anyway, you should kill Jolon. Swear it, and we part peaceably."

Kalen's stomach twisted in knots. The night he'd killed Revon had been the bloodiest of an already bloody life. It had almost cost him everything from his life to his humanity. Years had passed before he pulled himself out of the hole his sins had dug. Killing Jolon risked too much. Sascha wouldn't make it to the tree on her own. He considered lying. Of giving his oath and breaking it as soon as he was in Kunama land. How different was it from breaking his last oath here and now? If anything, it would be more peaceful than fighting here.

"No," he said. "Sascha's life is all that matters."

Aryn's answering look was hard, but it only lasted for a moment. "I've missed having warriors like you around. Most in your place would have sworn with abandon."

"There will be no lies between us. I'm suffering the cost of my omissions with Sascha every day."

Aryn nodded and looked away. "Does she know what's coming? You'll forgive my ignorance, but I don't know Vilkas's initiation rites. I imagine they're... unpleasant."

Kalen's throat constricted. "Never in a thousand lifetimes would I want to see my child subjected to them."

"I see. I'm sorry, friend." She fell silent as she considered her predicament.

"You put me in a difficult position," she said.

"Blame Vilkas. He fought Bonde to claim Sascha. If not for his refusal to die, none of this would have come to pass."

"I'm not so quick to accuse the gods," Aryn said, then sighed. "Fine. I release you from your oaths. But try not to be discovered anywhere near our border. I'm not sure I can stop you, but I know for damn sure I can't stop Jolon if he sets his sights on us."

Kalen bowed his head all the way to the floor of her tent. He held the position, silently thanking Aryn and all of Bonde's people for the kindness they'd shown him over the years. True, he'd paid for it, but they'd been good to him for a long time. "Don't worry. The wolf is only seen when it so desires."

IGNORANCE

Sascha hadn't gone far from Aryn's tent when she spotted Angar. She wasn't sure she wanted to talk to him now when what she most wanted was to find something to punch, but he saw her, too. She suspected he'd been waiting for her to emerge.

Her chest felt warm at the thought. She'd liked Rolf well enough, and he was a head and shoulders more interesting than anyone else within ten miles of the village. Angar, though, was a shining sun compared to Rolf's dim star. She'd always imagined warriors as brutish idiots that smelled like pig shit. Most who passed through her village fit the description well.

Angar was none of that. He was quick-witted and smiled easily. He listened to her stories like they weren't just the ramblings they were. When each story ended, he asked for another. He made her feel like the heart of the world in a way Rolf never had. The half-day she'd spent riding behind him had passed in the blink of an eye.

"Is the conversation already over?" he asked.

"No, but I'd heard enough."

Thankfully, he read her emotions well enough that he didn't press. "Would you care to take a walk around the camp? You said you've never been, right?"

"Right, and yes, I'd like that."

Angar's tour was exactly what she needed. He introduced her to many other warriors, who all seemed pleased to have a visitor. He explained some of the camp routines and answered her mundane questions about his life. His answers were long-winded, which she appreciated. Walking in silence gave her time to think, though she was no closer to finding answers.

Their tour led them well outside the camp, but Sascha didn't even realize it until they came to a stop.

"You look like a woman with something on her mind," Angar said.

"I'm sorry. I'm afraid I'm not very good company."

"Nonsense. After months of seeing the same faces, any visitor is welcome, and beautiful ones more than most."

Sascha recognized the flattery but appreciated it anyway.

"May I ask what troubles you?" Angar asked.

"Lots of things. You knew my dad. How?"

Angar looked at her like she was mad. "Your dad is a legend among warriors. Most probably wouldn't recognize him on sight these days, but I'd seen Fang before, so that helped."

"What did he do?"

"You don't know?"

Her silence was answer enough.

"I see." They walked for a while before Angar told the story.

"Remember, I was only a young man when I saw this,

and I'm sure my memory has exaggerated the events over the years. At the time, my mother wasn't a chief, but she was a powerful warrior in line for the position. She's always been among the best of our people.

"Your father came one winter, escorting your mother south. She was already heavy with you, and a host of opposing clans pursued them. Your father sought shelter, but Kline, our chief, wanted nothing to do with him. Bonde was already embattled and losing ground. Somehow, your parents convinced Kline's runemaster to cast for them."

Angar paused, deep in thought. "It astounds me sometimes how much that one cast changed the course of our people. The runes claimed your father had the strength to save us all. Kline was a cautious chief, though, humbled by loss after loss. He chose not to take the risk and send Kalen away. That was when Kalen drew Fang."

Angar stopped and looked back toward his mother's tent. "You need to understand. My mother was considered the best warrior Bonde had seen in generations. I grew up thinking she was invincible, and many of those who fought beside her felt the same. Kalen defeated her with ease. If you look closely, you can still see the scar on her neck where he threatened her life."

Sascha believed Angar spoke the truth, but she couldn't make the different versions of her father match. The man she knew had never once raised his hand in violence.

"The fight convinced Kline. He offered Kalen protection in exchange for the completion of an impossible task. If Kalen killed the leadership of the scorpions, we would grant him a home deep within Bonde's heart. Your father should have died, but he returned two weeks later, covered in blood and scars, Revon's head in his pack. He single-handedly came close to destroying a clan, and in return, he earned the life of peace he desired."

Sascha shook her head, not sure what to believe.

"He's never told you any of this? Or your mother?"

"No, and she died several years ago from illness."

"I'm sorry."

"Thanks." Sascha stared north, imagining an entire clan that wanted nothing more than her father's head.

"What will you do now that you know?"

Sascha shrugged. "How should I know? He's dragging me north because he believes he needs to, but I don't know what's best. I don't even know what's true right now."

"Have the runes told you anything?"

"I wouldn't know. Our local runemaster would never cast for me."

A sudden light shone in Angar's eyes. "I would cast for you, if you like."

"You have your own runes?"

"I do. Someday, I hope to take my mother's place as chief, so I've studied the art since I was a child."

Sascha hesitated. Sonje wasn't a fool or prone to panic, so if she'd refused to cast for Sascha, there was probably a good reason.

But Sascha knew now how small her world had been. Rolf was nothing compared to Angar, and Sonje herself had admitted she knew less about runes and casting than Kalen. The same was probably true of Angar. "Yes, please."

His smile reassured her. He offered his hand, which she took. He led her through the tents until they stopped at one closer to the center. The cookfire nearby blazed brightly as an attending warrior waited for it to burn down to coals. Angar opened the flap to his tent, and Sascha stepped inside.

Angar's dwellings were less ornate than his mother's. He had enough skins and blankets for warmth, but there was little else that caught Sascha's attention. He pulled out a small pouch, and she heard wooden runes clack within.

Her hesitation returned. Even Sonje had stone runes to cast, capable of channeling far greater powers. She saw no fear or worry on Angar's face, though, so she chided herself. They sat down across from one another, and Angar searched his tent for a handkerchief. Once he found a clean one, he laid it flat between them.

He took a small needle. "Do you want to, or should I?"

"You, please."

He gently took one of her hands in his own. She felt the callouses on his palm, but his grip was light. She was impressed. Rolf didn't know his own strength and often accidentally hurt her by squeezing too hard. She barely felt the prick on her finger, and he caught the blood with his runes. He collected enough to coat several, but her wound healed before he could cover them all.

He glanced at her and shrugged. "That should be enough."

He focused on the stones and shook them in his hand. As soon as he began to cast, the air in the tent changed. It grew cold as though a winter storm from the north had barged in through the open flap. Sascha's insides twisted, and she was glad she hadn't eaten yet.

She thought Angar would stop, but he continued to cast. His eyes were wide, but he was as determined to cast the runes as she imagined he would be in battle. When he thought he'd poured enough of his will into the process, he cast.

As he did, chaos erupted inside the tent. The cold air

became gelid, freezing her throat and lungs as she tried to breathe. The air around the runes distorted, knocking both her and Angar back. It felt as though someone had punched her hard in the stomach. As the runes settled, they smoked, her blood soaking into the wood and vanishing. The moment they came to rest, they caught on fire, burning brighter than the cookfire outside. The flames licked the top of the tent, but no warmth resulted.

Angar reacted with the speed and competence of a trained commander. He grabbed one of his furs and covered the fire, snuffing it out before it caused any more damage. Once it was out, his greatest concern was for her. "Are you hurt?"

She shook her head, unable to speak. Everything from the flame to the freezing air had vanished as quickly as it had appeared. Even the sudden pain in her stomach was no more.

Before they could talk about what happened, Aryn and Dad barged into the tent. "What did you do?" Aryn snapped.

Angar stood, prepared for his punishment. "I cast for her."

A look passed between the two older adults.

"Do the scorpions have any masters close to the border?" Kalen asked.

"A few. It would have been felt," Aryn answered.

"How long?" Kalen said.

"Two days, at most, before they arrive."

Sascha pushed herself to her feet, but she couldn't keep up with Aryn and Dad's discussion. Dad was deep in thought, though. After a bit, he spoke. "We can head northeast, and I'll draw their attention. If you shift your forces far enough to the west, you might avoid a fight."

Aryn was quick to accept. "We'll provision you as well as we're able. You've got a long journey ahead."

"I appreciate it. I'll do what I can to keep them off your backs," Dad replied.

The two bowed deeply to one another, then Aryn left the tent. Sascha heard her barking orders, and the camp leaped into action. The cookfire was extinguished, and warriors started removing their gear from tents. It took Sascha a bit for her thoughts to catch up to reality, but then she realized the warriors were leaving now.

If any had complaints about their evening of rest being cut short, Sascha didn't hear them. Then Dad moved deeper into the tent, bringing her attention back inside. Angar was pale and took half a step back. He didn't deserve to suffer one of her dad's tirades just because he'd tried to help. "Dad, can you leave? We're fine."

He ignored her and crouched down next to the blanket in the center of the tent. He lifted it from its corner as gently as he would pick up a newborn. Underneath, nothing remained of Angar's runes. The wooden carvings had burned completely to ash.

Dad grunted. "You tried to cast for my daughter with *wooden runes*?"

Sascha stepped forward, ready to shout him down if he lost his temper, but he just shook his head.

Dad stood. "You must have felt the power in her blood as you focused your will."

Angar nodded. His eyes kept darting down to Fang, still at Dad's hip.

"Let this be a lesson for you, boy. It's easy to forget the power of runes when you're casting for farmers and friends. Early success makes you confident. It's important never to lose your humility, though. Every rune represents the will of gods. When they shout, it's best to pay attention."

Angar nodded vigorously as though he'd never agreed with anything more passionately in his life.

That seemed good enough for Dad. "Hopefully, you won't have to pay too high a price for your pride tonight. You've got promise, boy. Don't let it go to your head."

Dad turned his attention to her. "Say your farewells. We need to leave soon."

With that, he strode from the tent.

Sascha looked from Angar to her father's departing figure. Angar looked half his age, cut down by Dad's cruel words. She clenched her fists. "I'll be back," she said. Then she followed her father.

"Dad!"

He stopped and turned, but he didn't look surprised to be accosted. "Yes?"

"He was only trying to help!"

"I know."

"So, why do we have to leave? Why are they packing up to flee?"

Dad's gaze hardened, but he controlled his anger. The gaze of others had always tempered his worst outbursts. He was more ashamed of looking bad in front of neighbors than he was of his own anger. "Haven't you been listening? The clan chief of the scorpions wants my head, and thanks to you and Angar, he'll soon know exactly where I am."

"But Angar was casting for me!"

"Sure, but to get that powerful of a reaction, he must have used a fair amount of your blood. And although you might not like the fact, half of your blood came from me.

That's one reason I never let Sonje cast for you, and when she did, she used only a small dab of your blood."

"I don't want to go. I feel safer here."

She expected an outburst, but her father surprised her. He sighed, then stared at her. She didn't flinch away. "Do you believe that Sonje and I speak the truth? That you've been called by Vilkas, and if you refuse to answer the call, you'll soon die?"

Until a few days ago, Sascha would have claimed Dad had never lied to her. The same was true of Sonje. From one perspective, he still never had. He'd just never spoken about his past.

She hated to admit it, but she believed his story. "I do."

Dad breathed in deeply. She thought he looked afraid, though she'd never seen the expression on his face before. "Then I'll leave the decision to you. After tonight, I'm not sure we could return home. But we could settle someplace else for the months you have left. If you wanted, we could even travel with these warriors. It was unfair of me to pull you along without giving you a choice. I only knew I would do anything to keep you alive. What would you have us do?"

She shifted her weight from one foot to the other. "What would happen if we stayed with the warriors?"

"I would still have to leave for a few days to pull attention away from them. Then we could travel with them as long as your health allows. You'd be dead by year's end." His voice was flat and hard.

It wasn't really a choice, but she hesitated. Ultimately, though, her desire to live won out. "Let's go north."

Dad's relief was immediate and obvious. "That's good. I'll finish our preparations if you want to speak with Angar. The boy likes you."

"He's not a boy."

Dad snorted. "When you've seen as many years as I have, he still seems like one. Go on. I'll see you soon."

When Sascha returned to the tent, Angar had recovered some of his color. She found him brushing the ashes from his tent and preparing to leave. "I'm sorry," she said.

Some of his cheer had returned, though he was still shaken. "There's nothing to apologize for. You couldn't have known, and I should have known better."

"Can I help you?"

Angar accepted the offer and gave her directions. Before long, his tent was empty and ready to be dismantled. By the time they should have been eating supper, tents were already coming down. Her own stomach rumbled at the thought. "I'm also sorry you don't get to rest tonight."

He shrugged. "Happens more often than any of us like, but it's part of the life we agreed to. They'll give me grief when they find I'm the cause, though."

"Take care of yourself until I return," Sascha said.

Angar gave her a grim smile. "Lies don't become you. I hope our paths cross again someday, but I suspect that day will be long in coming, if ever. I'm the warrior, yet your life is in far more danger than mine. You should be the one taking care of yourself."

Sascha nodded, then felt a lump in her throat. "Thank you for today. I—appreciated your company."

Angar gave her an elegant bow. "I hope I remember you as long as I did your father, but I hope I see you much sooner."

They parted, Angar to his tasks and Sascha to find her father. She found him speaking with Aryn, two full packs resting by his feet. They were discussing the details of their plan when she joined them.

"I'm sorry it came to this," Aryn said. "Your task was difficult enough as it was."

"What's done is done, and it doesn't change our destination. I shoulder as much blame as anyone here. I should have told Sascha more about who she is."

"May the gods go with you," Aryn said.

Dad picked up his pack and passed the other to Sascha. "Somehow, I have the feeling their meddling fingers already have us all in their grasp."

ANCIENT FRIENDS

Kalen knew his daughter was exhausted and knew she was too proud and stubborn to say anything about it. She'd ridden with Angar most of the day, but riding wore the body down, too, just in different ways. Not only that, but they'd had no true rest since. He'd hoped for a warm meal and shelter at the camp, but life had a way of taking one's hopes and smashing them against the ground.

He wasn't sure when they'd crossed the border, but he was certain they were in enemy territory. There were fewer fields here, and those they passed were choked full of weeds. Not a single grain of wheat had been harvested. The scorpions were sitting on a treasure, but they'd let it rot in their ignorance.

His gaze searched the horizon for a place to hide Sascha for a day. He knew how to pull the scorpions' attention away from Bonde's warriors, but there was little chance of him succeeding if she accompanied him. He needed to strike fast and vanish after.

Unfortunately, the prairie provided few promising options.

Most groves of trees were near water, making them prime rests for any groups of warriors seeking respite. As he grew more desperate, he considered planting her in the middle of a field and hoping for the best, but he couldn't stomach the risk.

Sascha tripped over her own feet. He glanced back, but she waved away his concern. Still, he slowed until he walked beside her. "Sonje taught you some of Bonde's basic runes, right? Even though I asked her not to?"

Sascha's focused stare at her feet was answer enough.

"Would you like me to teach you one of Vilkas's runes?"

Her eyes shot up. "You would do that?"

He wanted to say no, that the last thing he wanted to do was give her the same strength that had brought him so much grief. But he couldn't protect her forever, and she'd need some skill with runes if she hoped to survive her initiation. "I would."

She nodded, and the weariness fell from her shoulders.

Her eagerness brought a smile to his face. Once, he'd craved the same knowledge. "Vilkas has one rune we can use tonight. Like all runes, it doesn't have a specific meaning. The concepts of the gods don't always translate well to our world."

Her eyes were dull, and he realized Sonje had probably already lectured her on all of this. He dove straight to the point. "This word means something akin to 'endurance.' It's the ability to keep going long after the body should rest."

"Like what you used earlier today?"

"Exactly. This is the sound of the rune, so listen close." Careful not to put any will into the rune, he spoke it out loud. He'd always thought of it as the sound of a wolf trotting through the woods.

She tried to repeat it, and he corrected her tone. Then she had it. He shook his head. She learned as fast as Embla had.

"Now, focus your will on the idea of running forever, of a patient strength that never fades. Imagine pushing that will into the word, then whisper it, so your enemies won't know your plans."

She concentrated and spoke. Her back straightened, and her pace quickened. Her eyes widened, and she looked at her hands as though they belonged to a stranger.

Her amazement brought a smile to his lips. He'd had good reason to resist teaching her any of Vilkas's runes, but he'd always imagined she'd be a quick study. Her achievement wasn't much, but he was proud of her all the same.

"It is wise not to use the rune too often," he cautioned. "It restores strength and increases endurance, but it is no substitute for a full night's sleep, a hearty meal, and regular physical training."

She nodded without truly hearing his warning. He couldn't fault her. He'd been much the same in his heady younger days. Some lessons could only be taught through suffering the consequences.

They summited a small rise in the land and came upon the ruins of a village. Given that they were still surrounded by untended fields, Kalen guessed the scorpions had conquered this land earlier this summer.

Kalen dropped into a squat and motioned for Sascha to do the same. They didn't have many hours before the rising of the sun, and there was much to do. He watched the ruins for a time. Nothing moved within. They would be good enough for the day. He stood and walked toward the village, Sascha close on his heels.

The village was smaller than Lysabel's, being farther from Bonde's heart, but the homes were the same basic design as his and his neighbors'. A few had been burned. Kalen explored one of the unharmed homes. The interior had been thoroughly searched by the invaders, but he didn't care to leave Sascha in a room full of corpses.

He hadn't spoken of his plans, and there was no easy way to tell her, so he just told her the truth. "I need to leave you here for a while, but I should be back before nightfall."

He would have done anything to take the hurt in her eyes away from her, but that hurt and fear turned to anger in the space of a heartbeat. "You can't just leave me here! Wherever you go, I'll follow. I can keep up."

"It's not about that. I need to draw the attention away from Aryn's warriors. To do that, I'll make a scene that's going to draw every scorpion for a dozen miles. I can't have you anywhere near when that happens."

He watched reason and emotion war across her face. "What if scorpions come here?"

Kalen gestured around the house. "They didn't camp here tonight, and there's nothing in the village worth taking. There aren't many reasons for them to stop."

She wasn't convinced, and she probably had the right of it. But he couldn't bring her with him, and this was as safe a place as they'd found. His desire to repay Bonde's kindness and keep his daughter protected conflicted and there was no simple answer.

Although she'd used the previous rune with such ease, perhaps he could teach her another. "What if I give you a tool to help you protect yourself?"

Her eyes lit up. "Another rune?"

He nodded.

She made a show of deliberating, but she was hooked like an overeager fish in the trout stream outside their village. "Fine. What's the rune?"

"It's a rune of hiding. You know how many animals blend with their surroundings? It's like that. You aren't invisible, exactly, but gazes won't linger in your direction. Most will pass right over you without stopping."

"Most?"

"It's not perfect. Just as a sharp eye can spot an animal in the woods, it can spot you despite the rune's power. Fear not, though, as most people aren't too observant, and the more you do to hide yourself, the stronger the effect."

Once again, Kalen taught her the word. When she had the pronunciation close enough, he told her to channel her will into the word, to imagine hiding.

The rune didn't hide her from his sight, but he felt his eyes' desire to look elsewhere, which told him she'd cast the rune successfully.

"Did Sonje teach you much about channeling your will into a rune?"

Sascha shook her head.

"The effects of a rune are more powerful depending on the will you push into them. But that doesn't always mean stronger is better. An alert runemaster will sense when a rune is being invoked nearby. You did well just now. The runemaster would have had to be in the house with you to feel it. But control is harder when you're panicked, and novices often focus too much will into a rune when they're scared. If you see someone coming, hide yourself well and use the rune long before they arrive. Preparation often defeats skill."

There would never be a better time to leave. With luck, he could put ten miles behind him before the sun rose. "Will you be fine for a day?"

Her uncertainty hadn't faded completely, but she nodded.

"I'll be back before nightfall. I promise."

"And if you're not?"

He didn't have an appropriate answer for her, and she knew it.

"That's what I thought," she spat. She waved him away. "Go. I'll be fine."

Kalen searched for something that would heal the new rift between them, but he found nothing. "I love you so much."

She grunted and turned from him.

Kalen balled his hands into fists, then left the house, village, and daughter behind.

He'd barely run a mile when he noticed he had company. He glanced to his left and saw an old man keeping pace without a problem.

Kalen growled.

"It's been a long time, old friend," the old man said.

"Not long enough."

"No gratitude? I'm hurt."

Kalen stopped and turned, ready to drive his fist into the old man's face. But the visitor wasn't there. He heard laughter behind him and spun. The old man stood, hands in the pockets of his ragged pants, a confident smile on his face.

His teeth were too bright in the last reflected light of the moon. "You've still got that anger, though."

"What are you doing here?"

"Nowhere else to go. Nowhere else I'd rather be. You might have forgotten your vows, but I'll keep mine until the end of time. You'll need me for what's to come."

Kalen snarled. "If not for you, we wouldn't be in this damned mess. She could have had a peaceful life."

"The wolf belongs with its pack," Vilkas said.

"There is no more pack! They hunted us to the ends of this world, and I'm the last that remains. You just couldn't fade peacefully."

Kalen considered drawing Fang, and Vilkas took a step back. Something in Kalen's posture must have warned him.

"You think you can kill me, where even my brothers and sisters have failed?" the old man asked.

"Was thinking of trying it. *Can* Fang kill you?"

"I'd rather not find out."

Vilkas made no aggressive moves, and in time, Kalen mastered the fire that burned in his chest. "Why?" he asked.

"The world needs her, just as it once needed you."

"Nonsense! This is all about you."

Vilkas shook his head. "Once, it might have been. But these last few decades have given me time to reflect. Time to change, if such a thing is possible. I don't know if I can die, but I fade. My time of strength is long past, but perhaps enough remains to make a difference for those who will come after. Bonde grows in strength, but he's still weak as a babe. He has no appetite for blood. He needs to be defended until he can protect himself. Sascha can be that shield."

"She was supposed to live in peace!"

To cool his building rage, Kalen returned to running. He would not kill Vilkas, no matter how strong his desire, and time was wasting. Vilkas ran beside him.

"Is that what she wants? Or is that your dream, dumped on her?"

"Of course it's what she wants!"

"Perhaps you should ask her the next time you see her."

Kalen glared, and Vilkas wisely shut his mouth.

After another mile, the conniving god asked a very different question. "Where are you going?"

"You know where."

"Will you draw Fang?"

"Not if I can help it."

"Jolon will still know it's you."

"That's the point."

Vilkas was silent for a while, then said, "You don't owe Bonde anything. You paid for your peace with a river of blood. No more is required, and this will only make the journey more difficult. Far better to arrive safe and return than risk it all now."

"It's my fault Sascha didn't know better. My fault Aryn is in danger. Can't let that stand."

Vilkas nodded. He didn't seem displeased Kalen couldn't be swayed. "If you need me, you know how to call. I won't be far."

Then he was gone, and Kalen ran alone. Vilkas had given him plenty to consider, but now wasn't the time. Dawn broke on the eastern horizon, forcing him to move with greater care. He neared the old boundary of the scorpion's land.

He reached the stream midmorning. Thankfully, it was low, and he found a shallow stretch he could cross with little difficulty. Once on the other side, he continued east, farther away from both Sascha and Aryn. He saw no patrols nor any camps. From Aryn's information, he guessed most scorpions were gathered near the borders, pushing them ever outward.

He found what he was looking for before noon.

Part shrine, part boundary marker, it sent a shiver down his spine when he looked at it. Carved from a solid chunk of oak, the post was buried in the ground about twenty paces from the north edge of the stream. The lower part was rounded and carved with Kunama's runes. Kalen recognized some, similar enough to runes he knew better. He saw runes of protection, prosperity, and good hunting. Others were less familiar. Higher up, four scorpions, all standing with their backs to one another, had been delicately carved. They were vicious-looking creatures with fearsome glares, endlessly staring in all four directions.

Kalen took a deep breath. Drawing Fang would have made the task the work of a moment, but he feared what would result if he did. He spoke a complex phrase.

Before, he'd feared he'd lost some of his skill, so long unused. But the runes slid from his lips with ease. He spun and kicked at the pole. The runes carved upon it flared with power, and Vilkas and Kunama came into conflict for the first time in a generation.

A crack split the air and the pole, but the pole stood.

Kalen watched for a moment, waiting to see if he'd done anything besides split it. Already, every runemaster the scorpions had within miles would know what had happened. His task was completed, but not the way Kalen wished.

He spoke and kicked again. The wards flared but couldn't protect the pole from Kalen's strike. The guardian splintered into hundreds of pieces, some flying dozens of feet before coming to rest in the tall grass.

For good measure, Kalen pulled down his pants and pissed on the lower part of the pole. Once he was sure he was empty, he allowed himself a bit of a smile.

He liked to tell himself he'd put his old self behind when he'd moved to Bonde's lands, but he couldn't deny the pleasure of defiling the scorpions' boundary marker. A part of him had been missing all these years, and he'd just welcomed it back with open arms.

He didn't admire his work for long. Scorpions would be here soon, revenge the only thing on their small minds. He made a deliberate trail that continued east.

It wouldn't do to have the scorpions finding him and Sascha. Not when there was so much ground still to cover.

He laughed as he ran, feeling more alive than he had in years.

FIRST STEPS

Sascha waited in the house until he was out of sight. The house reminded her eerily of home. The front door opened into the main room, with a cookfire, table, and chairs. This table was longer than the one she'd grown up with, and more chairs were scattered around the room. Across from the front door was a dividing wall with two interior doors. Each led to a bedroom. The bedroom on her left held a bed large enough for two, and the other room had four smaller beds bunked in sets of two. A small doll had been abandoned in the second room, and Sascha tried hard not to think about what had happened to the doll's owner.

The truth was obvious, but every time her thoughts came too close to imagining the event, her heart raced so hard she thought she might collapse.

She was no fool. Raids on villages were a common enough occurrence, and word of such raids spread quickly across Bonde's land. She knew they happened, but they also felt far away, something that would never touch her.

Lysabel's village was always peaceful, and she'd grown up believing that was normal.

Sascha stood one chair up and slumped into it. She'd never admit as much to Dad, but she wanted to turn around and run back to Lysabel's village. She'd bury her head in her own blankets and wait for morning, praying this was all a dream.

She ran her right thumb across the pads of her other fingers and focused on the sensations. Her heart slowed.

Before long, boredom set in. Dad wanted her to stay hidden, but the sun wasn't up yet, and she might learn more about the fate of the villagers if she explored the remaining homes. She stood and left the house.

As soon as she stepped into the next intact home, she wished she hadn't. She found no bodies, but dried blood was splattered across the walls and floor. She ran out, slamming the door behind her. In the dead silence of the village, the echo made her jump. She hurried back to the first house.

Bored was good.

She didn't mind being bored at all.

She sat down in the chair, closed her eyes, and tried to wipe the thoughts of the other house from her memory. The harder she tried, the more vivid they became. She opened her eyes and, for a moment, thought the blood had seeped into this house as well. She blinked rapidly, and the nightmares faded.

Movement out of the corner of her eye made her jump again. She stood and went to the door. On the western horizon, she spotted a pair of figures walking toward the village. Soon they were joined by two more and another four after that.

Sascha swore. It was too dim, and they were too far away

for her to make out details, but her only reasonable guess was a hunting party of scorpions. She considered running, but they had a clear view of the door. She slunk back into the shadows and looked for a place to hide.

Her anger at Dad flared, consuming her fears while she searched. He'd promised she'd have nothing to worry about. She thought of the bloody room and the abandoned doll, and her legs almost gave out.

She collapsed to her knees, and her heart pounded in her chest so loudly she was sure the approaching hunting party would hear it. Her breath came in short, shallow gasps, and she crawled across the floor to the master bedroom.

Once there, she pulled herself up the doorframe, then leaned against it for support. The only place in the master bedroom to hide was under the bed, but she dismissed the idea. If this had been one of her childhood games of hide and seek, under that bed would be the first place she'd check.

She slid across the wall, not trusting her legs with her full weight. The only other place to hide was in the other room under the bunk beds. The shadows were smaller, but there was enough space for her to curl in tight. It wasn't great, but it was better than anyplace else in the house.

She fell to her knees and crawled across the room, then squeezed under one of the bunk beds. It was a tight fit, but the darkness provided some small comfort. Her heart raced, making concentration nearly impossible.

The scorpions couldn't be that far away, though. She imagined being invisible underneath the bed, concentrating her will and desire for safety into the rune. A moment before she spoke, Dad's warning came back to her. She tried to remember what it had felt like when she'd used the rune earlier, tried to reduce the will she channeled into the rune.

Then she whispered.

From her perspective, little happened. But her heart calmed, and she felt safe, as though someone had come and pulled a blanket over her. She kept imagining hiding, trickling her will into the rune to keep it active.

It wasn't long before she heard voices carrying through the open doors. They grew louder, their language one she'd not heard before. Their words sounded sharp, as though they were cutting one another with barbs and insults.

Though for all she knew, they were talking about how pleasant the weather was.

The floorboards creaked as at least two of the scorpions entered. A deep voice spoke, answered by the voice of a younger woman. Sascha heard laughter, and the footsteps went into the master bedroom. The door to the other bedroom closed, and there was more laughter, followed by the sound of weapons dropping to the floor.

Other sounds drifted through the walls, and Sascha was doubly glad she hadn't chosen to hide under the master bed.

Her satisfaction only lasted until she heard more footsteps in the house, followed by the sounds of soft conversation. Two more scorpions, if she had to guess. They kicked around the furniture in the main room, and one laughed in response to something the other said. Two men, then.

She held her breath as they stepped into the bunkroom. Distracted, she almost let her focus slip. She squeezed her eyes shut and made the rune the only focus in her life. She felt it working, like folding another layer of blanket on top of her.

The two men came deeper into the room, and she opened her eyes. A hand, covered in mud and blood, reached down to pick the doll off the floor. The hand's owner grunted, then tossed the doll under the bed, close to where Sascha hid. Then, as if regretting the decision, the hand reached to pull the sheets from the bed.

Sascha stopped breathing as a hard pair of eyes appeared. They glanced quickly around, passing over Sascha as if she wasn't there. They disappeared, and the hand holding the cover dropped. Before Sascha dared to breathe, the bunk bent as the warrior flopped upon it.

She almost let out a squeak. She pressed her lips tight together and let a trickle of air in through her nose.

On the opposite side of the small room, the second warrior lay on the other bottom bunk. They spoke for a bit before dozing off. In the other room, the sounds continued for some time longer before falling silent.

Sascha cursed her father again, imagining the various ways she'd seek revenge when he returned. She'd been silly enough to believe him when he said no one would stop and rest during the day, but these scorpions seemed like they'd had a long night. Maybe he hadn't lied, but he was a fool all the same, and she was the even greater one for listening.

She debated escaping. She was mostly sure that everyone was asleep.

The plan didn't withstand much scrutiny. Other scorpions wandered the ruins. Even if she left the room without being discovered, where would she go? The scorpion had already looked under the bed, and her rune had hidden her. Though she could reach out and touch the sleeping warrior, she didn't think anywhere else was safer.

She closed her eyes and brought her attention to her

breath and to the rune she powered. To keep it active, she kept funneling her will into it, imagining her hiding. It would last as long as she could. With Sonje, she'd never held a rune for long. Already she was well past what she'd attempted before, and there was much longer to go.

Perhaps she could let it go, but she didn't trust herself to speak the rune successfully again.

The challenge of the task became her sole focus. Her foolish father, the sleeping scorpions, and her own fear faded away like mist before the morning sun. Powering the rune became harder. She struggled, squeezing her eyes shut tight and concentrating until sweat dripped from her brow. She was sure she was about to lose her hold.

Then something shifted, and she felt a tremendous ease. Before, she'd imagined powering the rune as something akin to pushing, forcing her will into the rune. Now she felt it as a connection, her strength flowing into the rune like water poured gently from a pitcher.

She could maintain the connection as long as she remained awake.

Time lost meaning. Then, before noon, someone ran into the main room and shouted.

The scorpions were on their feet in moments. They shouted at one another and growled, but they left the house before Sascha could guess what had happened.

Wisdom dictated she remain hidden under the bunk, but curiosity got the better of her. Vilkas's runes had protected her thus far, and she was more confident in them than ever. She slid out from under the bed and pushed herself to her feet. She felt strong like she could cut down a swath of forest in an afternoon.

Sascha kept her connection to the rune open and

stepped into the main room of the house. She went to the door and watched the scorpions hurrying farther east.

Motion beside her caught her attention. An old man leaned against the wall of the house. He hadn't been there a moment before. He watched the scorpions flee with a wide smile on his face. "Your father always had a certain—style— I appreciated."

He stretched, then inhaled deeply, as though he had his nose pressed to a flower. "Good to see him back."

Something about him was familiar, though she'd never seen him before. He smiled, and his teeth were bright and sharp. The sight spurred her memory. Realization followed soon after. "Vilkas."

"It's an impressive skill you're displaying. Though there's no need for it anymore." He gestured to the horizon, where the scorpions could no longer be seen.

"They may return."

Vilkas shook his head. "Not after what your father did. He destroyed one of their sacred border posts with his foot. 'Kicking a hornet's nest' doesn't come close to describing the attention he's focused on himself."

Sascha turned and stared at the old man. "You just appear whenever you feel like it? Whenever you want to manipulate us?"

"For the most part. Though, I doubt I'll be able to help for a while. Kunama will want blood for this, so it's best I stay away. Should you make it to my lands, I'll have the power to fight."

"Are you a god?"

Vilkas shrugged. "So they say."

"Why are you here?"

Vilkas smiled, but his predatory teeth put her on edge. "To help, of course."

"Every time you help, my life gets upended."

"You always said you wanted more excitement. Don't complain when it happens."

She stepped toward him and stabbed a finger into his chest. "Have you been watching me for all these years?"

"I protect my people, Sascha, even when they don't know they're my people."

She snarled and turned away so she wouldn't have to look at him. "You lie!"

"I will only lie once to you, and when that time comes, it will be for a good reason. Otherwise, you can always count on me to tell you the truth. Right now, Kunama is no fool and has learned much since we last clashed. He suspects there is more to your father's actions than appearances suggest. Already he is summoning warriors back to the heart of his lands, ready to strike wherever you appear. The most direct routes to your homelands will be the most dangerous."

"Why don't you tell my father this?"

"Kalen has too much attention on him. If I were to appear anywhere near, Kunama himself would come for me."

"Why not fight him and be done with it?"

"Because I'm weak. The last true surviving blood of my clan is a man who would just as soon see me dead. Where there is no belief, there is no strength."

"Then maybe you should just die."

Part of her couldn't believe the words coming from her lips. Growing up, Bonde had been more of an idea than a reality, and she was coming to believe that was how she preferred her gods.

Thankfully, Vilkas took no offense. "You two are too similar. And perhaps right. Who am I to say? All I know is that if no one stands up to Kunama, this world will burn, and many will die. Look around you if you don't believe."

For the first time, Sascha found herself in the uncomfortable position of agreeing with Vilkas. The scorpions had done this, and she'd heard no grief or regret from those who'd slept in the house. "What can I do? My father never even saw fit to teach me the sword."

"No, but you're skilled with the bow. Even more important, you've shown a skill with my runes that is uncommon. You sense already the connection between you and the runes, don't you?"

She nodded, hating how eager she probably looked.

"You've already discovered the secret, and on your own, no less. Now that you've found it, pursue it. Follow it to the end, and you'll have abilities beyond your wildest imaginings."

"Will I be stronger than my father?"

"Perhaps. There's no telling."

She blinked, and Vilkas was suddenly by her side. "One warning. A trap many promising young students fall into. It's easy, when you've mastered a skill few others have, to think you're special. You're not, though. Unique, but never special. Anyone could do what you'll learn. It's just that most don't look. Most don't examine deeper if they don't have to. Keep searching and stay humble. Who knows what will happen?"

With that, he was gone, as though she'd imagined the entire scene. Unlike the time before, she remembered every word.

She cut off her connection with the rune, and the blankets she wrapped around her fell. The air felt suddenly cooler, and she shivered.

To be sure, she whispered the rune and the connection opened just like it had before.

She expected she would impress her father when he returned.

GUIDE

After he'd traveled a few miles, Kalen turned, so he was traveling west. The journey carried him deeper into scorpion territory, but compared to what he'd just done, the danger wasn't anything to lose sleep over. The route also gave him time to scout the land and get a sense of what life was like deep within the boundaries of Kunama's territory.

He saw few signs of settlement, though that didn't surprise him. Scorpions saw the crops and villages of Bonde's people as a foolish weakness. There were those, Kalen well knew, who considered Bonde's way of life an affront to their own, an open challenge that demanded answer. Regardless, he'd stumble upon no village or fields here. But he saw few human tracks, either. The land was wide open and empty.

He found plenty of game, though. Kunama's land was transitional, sitting between Bonde's farmlands and the higher, rougher altitudes of the mountain clans. Here, Kalen walked through ancient grasslands that stretched as far as the eye could see. Wind blew the grass in waves, and deer bounded far ahead of him.

He noted that there was plenty of game for the scorpions if they hunted it. Not that he needed the confirmation, but it proved that the scorpion's conquest wasn't about need but desire.

He covered his own tracks well, and only once did he come upon a scorpion hunting party. He whispered, using the same rune he'd taught Sascha to conceal himself as he squatted lower in the grass. The party had a runemaster among them, but they still passed within several hundred paces without noticing him. Their passage allowed Kalen to study them carefully.

All looked prepared for violence. They carried bows and swords of various makes, plunder from their raids. A few smelled of blood.

What most stood out to him, though, was how young they all looked. Some had to be younger than Sascha. They might have some battle experience. By their age, Kalen had already been building his legend. But they didn't strike him as truly dangerous. Their runemaster, in particular, seemed a weak practitioner. He didn't so much as glance in Kalen's direction.

Were they that young, or was he becoming that old? And were these warriors representative of Kunama's champions, or were these the weakest, banished to the south to hunt easy prey until they could prove useful in the more difficult fighting to the north and east?

He supposed he'd find out soon enough.

He hurried back to the village where he'd left Sascha, arriving well before the setting of the sun. He found her in the same house he'd left her, checking the fletching on her arrows. Right away, he sensed that something had changed.

A fresh smell lingered in the room, one that hadn't been there before. It smelled of sex and dirt, and his heart jumped into his throat as he thought of what might have happened to Sascha in his absence. "Was someone here?"

"Good to see you, too, and yes, I'm fine," she spat.

After a full day of running and hiding from patrols, Kalen was in no mood to deal with his daughter's attitude. But something had transpired here, and it had affected Sascha deeply. He also recognized a battlefield when he saw one. He might not know what forces were arrayed against him or understand the contours of the land, but he knew to proceed with caution.

Standing made him want to pace, so he sat down cross-legged in front of Sascha. "I'm sorry. It's been a long day for me, too. What happened?"

Sascha finished with one arrow and picked up the next. She ran her thumb lightly over the fletching, her gaze focused. He saw how she used the task to keep her anger in check, and he was once again reminded of the fact that so many in the village had told him before.

She was so much like him. Too much, perhaps.

When she had mastered her anger, she put down the arrow and looked at him. "You said that I would be safe. You said that no one would come here."

Her words dripped with venom. Kalen immediately understood what had happened. It might have even been the hunting party he'd passed earlier. And she'd been here, alone. He almost leaped to his feet to search for any of the hunting party who remained. But his daughter's calm behavior kept him rooted firmly in place.

"They came?"

She nodded. "One couple went into the master bedroom. Others climbed into the bunks where I was hiding, laying on top of me all morning." She paused and picked up an arrow. "You said that no one was supposed to be here."

His first instinct was to argue, to tell her there was no way he could have known. He had believed she was safe here. He wouldn't have dreamed of leaving her if that hadn't been true. Yet he'd been wrong. And what had happened had happened.

Kalen took a deep breath. She probably couldn't understand yet, but somewhere deep within her, she knew he hadn't tricked her. He hadn't purposely put her in harm's way. She couldn't see that yet, and that was fine. Right now, she was mad because he had left her, and danger had come. He hadn't been there when she needed him most. She had every right to be furious.

"They didn't find you." Half a statement and half a question, he invited her to tell him more.

Most days, she refused such invitations. Today she spoke with a quiet confidence he rarely heard from her. "I spoke the rune just as you taught me. One of them peeked under the bed and didn't see me."

Despite the danger she'd been in, his first reaction was one of pride. The training he'd provided was bare. To use one of Vilkas's runes while hiding from a hunting party was no small feat, even for an experienced warrior.

It forced him to consider Sascha in a new light. Mostly, he'd not tried to teach her Vilkas's runes because he was prepared for the secrets of the old wolf to die with him. But a small part of his reason was a doubt she had the patience and will necessary to make anything of his teachings. It was dangerous to dabble with the power of runes, as young Angar had recently discovered. He hadn't trusted her with them.

Maybe that had been a mistake. If so, it was best to own up to it quickly. "I'm impressed, girl."

Her nostrils flared, confusing Kalen for several long moments. When the realization hit, it was like a slap to the face. He almost laughed, except Sascha would have taken it poorly. No wonder she so often got angry when they spoke. "You hate it when I call you 'girl,' don't you?"

"Of course I do! I've seen sixteen summers, Dad." She spoke it like it was the most obvious fact in the world, and perhaps she was right about that, too. Observant as he considered himself, he often felt blind when his daughter was involved.

"Sorry, gir—Sascha. I don't mean anything by it. I know you're getting older, and are more adult than I probably want to admit. Can't much help but think of you as my little girl, though. It's a hard habit to break, even though the evidence is standing before me every day."

She glared at him for a while longer, but eventually, she softened. He figured that was as close as he was coming to an apology.

He filled in the silence. "Anyway, as I was saying, it's impressive what you could do. Keeping your will focused when everything is going wrong around you is one of the hardest things. I've seen a lot of warriors older and more experienced than you falter when it gets tough."

She wasn't done with her surprises. "Spoke to Vilkas, too. Figured out it was him in the grove that pointed me toward Fang."

"Figured as much. What did he have to say?"

"That you'd kicked the mother of all hornet's nests. Said he wasn't sure how much help he'd be until we reached the border. Left me some advice on how to improve my runes."

"Did he, now?" Kalen understood why the old man had disappeared. If Vilkas had been present when Kalen learned he was teaching Sascha runes, Kalen would have had his hands around that scrawny neck, testing Vilkas's belief that he couldn't die.

Too late, he realized Sascha was watching him closely. She asked, "Why does that make you so angry? He helped me. Helped us."

"Never wanted any of this for you, girl."

It was the wrong thing to say. She leaped to her feet and stormed out of the house before Kalen could reach out and stop her. He growled as she fled and pushed himself to his feet, preparing to chase her. He stopped after one stride.

They weren't going to fix what was broken between them by shouting. He hated himself for every time he raised his voice against her. Sure, his shouts left fewer bruises than his hand, but they wounded all the same.

She deserved better.

He breathed the anger out and found his center. When he'd been younger, he'd walked through the worst battles of his generation without doubt. Killing and dying were all the same to him, and neither touched him. Gods had cursed his name, and he'd never broken his stride.

Embla had been the first to make him lose his center. He'd known women before her, but none had captured him as effortlessly as she snared him. He'd considered himself a master of the hunt but had bowed before her.

Still, it wasn't until Sascha emerged from between Embla's legs that he understood the true meaning of chaos.

Not because raising Sascha had been particularly difficult but because the moment she was born, he'd loved her more than anything else in his life.

He and Embla had spoken about it frequently. Kalen loved Embla with his whole heart. Once bonded, he'd never known another woman, and he'd known none since she passed. He would have died in her place if he could have. When she became sick, he'd prayed to Vilkas and Bonde both, demanding and begging the gods to spare her and punish him instead. The gods all knew he was more than guilty enough for the slow and painful demise. They hadn't answered, but he'd prayed the same prayer until the day it no longer mattered.

Somehow, that love still paled in comparison to what he felt for Sascha. Embla had caused him to lose his balance, but Sascha had pushed him straight over, and Kalen didn't think he'd found his center since.

He craved that certainty he'd possessed when he was younger but had no idea how to find it again.

He pulled the pendant from under his tunic and rubbed it. It was warm to the touch, and he took strength from the small tree.

Sascha was too much like him. When he was her age, he'd already left his parents behind and had joined one of Vilkas's most renowned hunting parties. She yearned for the same freedom.

She didn't understand what that meant, though.

He rubbed at the pendant. Though he'd left his parents early, the hunting party had adopted him. How many times had they saved his life or taught him what he needed to survive?

It was his duty as a parent to prepare her for the freedom

she craved. If she wasn't ready, it was no one's fault but his own.

Kalen tucked the pendant back underneath his tunic, then went to find Sascha.

He found her leaning against one of the standing houses, her eyes closed. He stopped a few steps away, hoping she wouldn't run again. "I can't promise I'll never leave you again, but I'll do everything I can to keep us together from now on."

She nodded, but it looked more like an agreement to get him to go away than acceptance. He imagined that spending even more time with her father wasn't high on her list of desires at the moment.

"I'm also going to teach you more of Vilkas's runes," he said.

Her eyes snapped open. "Really?"

"As many as you can handle."

She pushed herself off the wall. "Why the change of heart?"

"What I said was true enough. I didn't want you to have any part of this, but none of the gods seemed to give a damn. I'd be an even bigger fool than you think I am to keep the knowledge from you now. Vilkas was right about me stirring up trouble, and I fear I won't be strong enough to protect you alone. So, I'm going to teach you what I probably should have years ago."

She was again watching him closely, but this time, she was satisfied by what she saw. "Good." She looked around the ruined village. "So, what do we do next?"

Finally, a question he was prepared for.

"We head north, towards home, and hope there isn't a whole army of scorpions in our way."

SPIRIT WALKER

Naga grinned as one of his strongest swords held off three other warriors. They were only armed with heavy sticks, but even those could kill if one took a blow to the head. All four combatants were drunk on the spirits of the village they'd just conquered, and their lack of balance and coordination showed. Naga's son, who had just seen his thirteenth summer, was probably the equal of the warriors in their current state.

What his warriors lacked in skill, they made up for in vigor and insults. Naga laughed as a blow missed completely, sending the offending warrior spinning to the ground.

It soon became clear that what had started as a diversion would last long into the night. The spirits had consumed the warriors, and there was more laughter than fighting.

He was tired. His party had hunted up and down the southern border of Kunama's lands. He was ready to return home to his wife and sons.

Soon. They sometimes struck out at Bonde during the winter, but the farmers were harder targets after the harvest was over. They gathered in their villages and couldn't be picked off as easily as when they worked the fields.

For the scorpion, winter was a time of rest. The young went through their initiation rites so they could hunt with the parties in the spring. They formed bonds in the cold winter nights when the sun fled their sky for warmer lands to the south. Joyful as the hunt was, it couldn't last year-round.

The first snow couldn't come fast enough. His body didn't recover from battles as it had when he was young. Then, he could hunt with his pack all day, drink all night, and be up first to fight the next morning. Now he stretched his aching limbs both when he woke and before he slept.

He rose and lifted his cup in honor of the combatants, drinking the last of the spirit with one long pull. It burned down his throat, and he welcomed the sensation. Bonde and his pathetic excuses for warriors weren't good for much, but their spirits were the best to ever coat his tongue.

He found his pack and wandered away from the fire. Most were already asleep, and he found a flat stretch where nothing poked his back. He stretched until his body felt loose, then lay down and slept.

Most of Naga's dreams were nightmares, but he'd long since grown used to them. When the nightmares stopped was when he paid attention.

He opened his eyes and found himself in a different world. Scents were sharper here, reminding him of when he was younger and could smell an enemy on the wind. The air smelled of pine, though no pines grew in sight. The sky was dark, and the land was covered in a dense mist that pushed against him when he walked.

The spirit world reminded him it didn't want him here. That he didn't belong.

He ignored its faint protests. His master pulled him through the tall grasses to a barren spot ahead. Naga followed the pull, though he had no other sense of his master.

When he stepped into the barren circle, the mist clinging to his legs fled. The sky brightened, the sun turning from a dark orb into a dim red light. After the darkness, his eyes needed a moment to adjust. Something, a cross between a shadow and a man, stood near the center of the circle. Naga recognized the feeling of his master, even though the form was unfamiliar. He hurried forward, bowing deep when he approached.

"Naga. You move faster here."

Naga held his bow, unsure of how to respond. His master pulled him into the spirit world often, but Naga claimed little familiarity with the strange realm.

Master didn't speak, leading Naga to believe he expected a response. "Yes, sir. The mist faded as soon as I stepped into the barren circle."

"I see. Rise, Naga."

He did. He tried to look at his master, but the figure was cloaked in shadows, preventing him from seeing clearly. Staring made his eyes hurt as the figure refused to focus before him. He'd never seen his master like this before.

"Why do you stare, warrior?"

Naga almost bowed his apology, but knew that would only anger his master more. Creating a path for those less skilled drained Master's strength, though it allowed them to speak over unimaginable distances. The truth was always fastest. "I have difficulty seeing you, Master. You are cloaked in shadows."

A sound, which might have been a grunt, came from the figure. It shifted to the side, and Naga thought it gestured toward the ground. "What do you see?"

Naga looked down, not sure what he was studying. There was a deep hole in the ground, though the hole itself wasn't wider than a post. Naga stepped closer and peered down the hole. He saw no bottom. A dead scorpion, larger than his foot, lay beside the hole.

He knew it for a test, but the answer wasn't apparent. He looked around, and his heart fell into his stomach.

Wolf prints surrounded them.

"Is it—"

"It is," Master finished for him. "He destroyed one of our ancestral poles earlier today."

"So, he's finally drawn Fang again?"

"He used his foot."

Naga didn't have to fake his anger. "It's no surprise he still walks the world, and without respect. But even for him, this is an affront."

"He seeks to draw my attention."

Naga frowned. "After all these years? Why?"

"I sensed the blood of his progeny. Someone was foolish enough to cast runes for it beside my borders."

"That makes no sense. He's hidden himself well."

"He's cooperating with Bonde. I do not know if he fled there or was simply passing through, but I believe they made a mistake. He hopes to keep my attention on him to spare Bonde."

Naga spit on the barren ground. Master would disapprove, but in the light of such stories, Naga couldn't help himself. "Sounds like the bastard. Honorable, right until the moment he isn't. Are you going to attack Bonde, anyway?"

"There's no need. Bonde will fall in due time. He believes he grows strong, but he's as weak as ever. My children could enslave him in a summer. There's no need to rush. Not when Kalen has shown himself."

"Do you know why?"

"I do not. I imagine to finish the work he started so many years ago."

That idea didn't sit right with Naga, but he knew better than to argue. Master wasn't a reasonable man where Kalen was involved. But then, few were, Naga included. For the first time in a decade, he dared to hope. "Master, why have you called me here?"

"I made you a promise, didn't I?"

"You did, master."

"Today, I fulfill it. Take your hunting party and hunt Kalen down. Bring his head to me, and I will raise you up as first among my warriors. You shall want for nothing."

"Your generosity has already humbled me, Master. You know this is the only thing I desire."

"Be careful your eagerness doesn't surpass the battle wisdom you've fought so hard to earn. He has yet to draw Fang, and he still possesses the strength to destroy powerfully runed guardians with his feet alone. Time, it seems, hasn't dulled his strength."

Naga bowed deeply. "You'll have his head, Master. I swear my oath to you."

Strength filled his limbs, and he felt strong. His master had blessed him. "Go then, warrior. Kunama watches over you and grants you his strength."

Naga left the barren circle and searched for wolf tracks. He found them fleeing to the west. He walked for a time, no more able to leave the spirit realm on his own as he could enter it. If he walked long enough, his master's influence would fade, and he'd drop back into the realms of mortal sleep.

The mist pressed against his legs as he walked, and his vision grew darker and darker. He fell into sleep, and for once, the nightmares of his past didn't disturb him.

He woke the next morning feeling stronger and more refreshed than most mornings. The same couldn't be said of many of his warriors, who clutched at their heads and shaded their eyes from any bright light.

Naga stood in the center of their camp and let his voice boom over the crowd louder than was necessary. He grinned as the warriors winced. They were fine warriors but too likely to lose themselves after a successful hunt. He needed them sharp for what was to come. They'd never gone after prey like this before. He explained what lay before them, the task that had come straight from the master himself. He lit a fire in their hearts, and he imagined that all the ghosts that haunted him were applauding, too.

The time had finally come.

Tracking and killing Kalen was going to be the hunt of his life.

RESCUE

Sascha couldn't remember enjoying learning anything more than learning about Vilkas's runes. Every night she and her dad woke near dusk. In those late hours, he taught her about her mind and how it was the key to unlocking incredible abilities. He taught her to find her center, that calm place in her mind where focus came easily. He'd often teach her a new rune, then they'd begin their journey for the night.

They made the most out of their time. As soon as the sky darkened, they resumed their trek north. With autumn around the corner, the nights were longer than the days, giving them plenty of hours to journey. Her task during those long hours was to practice the runes. Every night she began with the first rune he'd taught, then worked her way to the newest.

Dad spoke little, but that didn't mean he ignored her. Quite the opposite. He was always watching her progress, noting what she had mastered and what she struggled with. Even he had to admit there wasn't much of the latter, though. She picked up the runes like a young bird taking to flight. When Dad watched her, he watched with pride in his gaze, something she hadn't seen from him much these past years.

They ran into little trouble as they walked. Dad's senses were sharp, and he spotted camps and parties of scorpions long before they were noticed. There weren't many camps, though, and the vast majority of nights, they didn't spot another soul. Kunama controlled a vast land, and there were nights it seemed abandoned.

Sascha discovered she loved both being awake and traveling during the night. There was a stillness in the air as most animals and humans bedded down for sleep. The darkness wasn't perfect protection, but she felt safer knowing it was harder for the scorpions to spot her under the dim light of the stars and moon.

For several days, she convinced herself that all was right with the world. She and Dad had reached an unspoken truce, and when she lay down each morning, she looked forward to what the next night would bring.

Eventually, though, old grievances returned. She appreciated her father's lessons, but he doled out his knowledge like it was food that had to last throughout the winter. He never let her skip the first runes, even though she'd proven her mastery over them dozens of times. She was capable of much more, but he didn't push her as hard as he should have. One night she said as much, lashing out harder than she'd planned.

He didn't snap at her disrespect. She'd noticed that more frequently over the last few days. Despite their predicament, he was less agitated than he had been at home. The long nights and constant danger seemed to shave the edge off his anger. She still sensed it there, hiding underneath the surface of his skin like a snake preparing to uncoil, but it had become more patient of late. She liked the change.

When she challenged him, he said, "It's something I've been thinking about, too. You pick up new runes faster than most. What you've mastered on this journey took me the better part of a year, and I was considered gifted by the clan elders. If you think you can master more, I'll teach you two runes a night from now on. But I won't bend on practice. You must train everything you've learned every night. You use the runes well, but they aren't a part of you yet, and there's no shortcut to that."

It wasn't a perfect victory, but it was more than she'd expected, and it kept her content as they continued north.

Soon, their path brought them to a forest. Sascha's jaw dropped when she first saw it.

"It's one of two great forests on Kunama land," Dad said as he swept his arm across the vista. "This one stretches from here to Kunama's Great Camp, where Jolon most likely sits upon his throne. We'll pass through another one before we reach the northern border."

She'd imagined a forest as being a larger grove, but the comparison didn't do the forest justice. It stretched as far as her eye could see, and many of the trees reached higher than she'd thought possible. The thick canopy blocked much of the light from the moon and stars. She tripped over roots she couldn't see and once almost ran into a trunk.

The next night, Dad taught her runes to improve her vision. She didn't care to hold the rune in her mind throughout the entire night, but she used the runes whenever they crossed a darker section of trees.

Their routine was shattered one night when Dad called a stop to their endless walking.

"What?" she asked.

Dad sniffed the air and frowned, then shook his head. "Someone is following us."

Sascha spoke the runes that sharpened her vision and looked around. She couldn't see far, but the forest seemed unchanged. Owls hunted above while nocturnal creatures skittered around the forest floor, but she neither saw nor heard any sign of enemies.

"Stay here. I'll scout around," Dad said.

Sascha kept her voice low, even as she snapped at him. "No! You promised we would stay together."

Dad snarled but quickly mastered himself. "You're not ready for this."

"And I never will be if you don't teach me."

She thought he might lose his temper, but he surprised her again. He grimaced and relaxed. She saw what the effort cost him, but he nodded and said, "You're right."

He looked around again, then stepped next to her so his voice wouldn't carry. "I think there's at least two, but maybe more. They're both to the south. Use the runes to hide and follow close behind me. If anything happens and you lose track of me, stay where you are. It'll be easier for me to find you than the other way around."

She almost argued. After all her practice, she was as good as anyone else at hiding, including her father. She feared an argument would only lose her the privileges he was extending, though, so she kept her mouth shut. She'd show him.

"Ready?" he asked.

She nodded. He spoke under his breath, and though he was standing right before her, he vanished.

Sascha's eyes went wide. She looked left and right, but there wasn't a sign of him. She relaxed her gaze and let it roam, finding him just a few steps in front of her. His body had disappeared, but there was something slightly off about the space he occupied, a slight bending of straight lines few would notice. Once she spotted him, it wasn't too hard to track him. She could always find him in the place her eyes wanted to look away from.

She spoke the same rune and felt the familiar blanket of protection drape over her. She followed him as he went back down along the game trail they'd just been climbing. They walked long enough that she wondered if they were chasing ghosts. How could he have known they were being followed if their pursuers were this far back?

She found it hard to keep her will focused. They'd already been walking for half the night, and it was much harder to keep focused while walking through the woods. She sought her center, but it kept wobbling away from her.

Dad didn't have any of the same problems. He remained almost impossible to see, and his footsteps were too silent to hear, even as Sascha followed directly behind him. Despite her attention, she almost hit his back when he halted.

"Stay here. I'll return shortly, but you move too loud for this next part."

Before she could argue, he took a few steps forward and was gone. No matter what she did to find him, she couldn't spot him. She hissed, but there was nothing for her to do. She dropped into a squat and waited.

No sooner had she done so than she saw a flicker of firelight off to her right. Sascha turned her eyes that way and saw a young man and woman, not much older than her, working their way carefully through the woods. Both had swords drawn.

Her first instinct was to hide, but she ignored it. They were far enough away that they probably wouldn't see her even without the runes. Then her father's admonishment echoed in her ears. After all their training, he still didn't think she was capable. The only way to change his mind was to show him she could be useful, too.

She sought her center and found it with ease. Her will flowed smoothly into her rune. Only fear held her back.

She checked for her father one more time, then followed the light. She placed her feet carefully, avoiding sticks that would snap underfoot. Thankfully, the warriors with the torch weren't moving quickly. Soon she was close enough to hear them.

Their conversation didn't give her any extra information, though. They spoke the same dialect as the warriors from the ruined village, and Sascha couldn't guess what they discussed. They were eager, though. Whenever a creature fled from them, they pointed their swords and hissed.

As she stepped around a tree, a dark shadow separated from it and punched at her.

She'd been so confident in her runes she didn't even pay attention to the threat until it was too late. The punch landed awkwardly, but it still knocked her back into another tree. She grunted as the back of her head cracked into the trunk.

The shadow formed into the shape of a woman. Her hair was braided tightly, and her face had tattooed patterns that drew Sascha's gaze. As she stared, the woman snapped a kick that caught Sascha cleanly in the stomach. She doubled over, holding her arms tight around her torso. Too late, she realized she couldn't feel the comforting presence of the rune keeping her from sight. She tried to find her center and summon the rune again, but it was impossible when all she could think about was pulling air into her lungs. She remained standing, but her knees wobbled, and the world spun around her.

The new arrival spoke in the common tongue. "Impressive unsight, for one so clueless."

"How?" Sascha croaked. She knew it wasn't the most important question she should ask, but she didn't care.

The woman tapped her ear. "Loud."

Sascha straightened. Her stomach hurt, but if she didn't fight, she suspected she wouldn't see the sunrise. The woman had caught her by surprise, but she'd made the mistake of letting Sascha recover.

She found her center and whispered. The rune gave her strength, and she lashed out with her fist. The woman leaned back and let the fist pass harmlessly in front of her face. Sascha kicked, but the woman deflected it with her arm, throwing Sascha off-balance.

She stumbled back, only now noticing the other two warriors were watching. They didn't seem terribly concerned about their friend. Their swords rested on their shoulders.

Sascha swore. She'd show them once she dealt with this first woman. She spoke another rune, filling her arms with strength. This time she advanced carefully, leading with quick jabs. She hit nothing and, a moment later, was on her knees, clutching once again at her stomach. She hadn't seen the woman's boot before it struck, and it felt like a tree had landed on top of her.

When she could open her eyes, she saw the woman's

boot right in front of her face. "Lick my boot," the woman said, laughter in her voice, "and I'll end your pain. Otherwise, this is only the beginning."

Sascha spit at the boot, but the woman moved it too fast. The boot kicked her in the face, breaking her nose and lifting her gaze to the sky. Blood sprayed, and Sascha saw pinpoints of light dancing in her vision. Her only thought was that there shouldn't be stars underneath the canopy. She fell into the dirt, unable to move.

The woman spoke in the common tongue to the others. "Tie her up and take her to him. He'll want to meet her."

The other two moved toward Sascha. She watched. Throughout her life, she'd never considered herself an angry person. Insults slid off her, and rumors rarely wormed their way under her skin. Now, though, she wanted to kill all the scorpions.

Unfortunately, she couldn't get her limbs to answer her pleas. The scorpions advanced without a hint of fear as though she was no more dangerous than a heavy stone that needed to be moved. The woman squatted down beside her. "I gave you a chance, wolf."

She stood, and then suddenly, her feet left the ground. At first, Sascha thought the woman had jumped, but then the feet went flying back and away from her, which made no sense at all. As more of the woman came into view, Sascha saw the surprise on her face.

It was the woman's last expression. She was driven, head-first, into the trunk of a tree. In the battle between her skull and the gnarled oak, her skull lost. Blood, bone, and brain burst upon impact as her face was flattened.

Then Dad stood there, his right hand holding the

woman up by her shattered skull. When he let go, her body crumpled like a heavy rag.

The other two warriors brought their swords from their shoulders, but they looked slow compared to Dad. He put his weight into a punch that struck the young man square in the chest. Sascha heard the warrior's chest crack as his ribs caved in.

Dad stepped to the side as the woman cut down at him. Her sword missed as cleanly as Sascha's punches had earlier. He grabbed the scorpion's throat and picked her up, squeezing tight. "Who's leading you?"

The woman kicked at him, but he paid the strikes no mind. She raised the sword, but he slapped the arm away with disdain.

She swore at him and drew a knife with her other hand.

Dad dropped her as she stabbed, and her strike missed. She tried again, but his hand moved faster than Sascha could follow. He wrapped his hand around hers and redirected the blade, driving it into her skull under the chin. Her eyes rolled up in the back of her head as she fell.

Dad glanced at Sascha but didn't go to her. Instead, he checked on the young man, who was trying to crawl away. The young warrior was dead. His body just hadn't realized it yet. Dad grabbed the sword the young man had dropped and stabbed down with it, cutting the scorpion's heart in two and ending the young man's agony.

Only then did he turn to Sascha. His hands were covered in blood and worse, and she didn't want them anywhere near her. He didn't care, even as she grunted her displeasure. He turned her over, and though he was gentle, it felt as if he crushed her.

"Where does it hurt?" he asked.

"Everywhere," she croaked.

"Can you move?"

"Don't want to."

"We can't stay, girl. Can you move, or do I need to carry you?" As he asked, he leaned forward as if he was about to scoop her up and carry her.

"No!" she shouted, finally finding her breath. "Don't touch me with your bloody hands!"

Her voice was higher-pitched and more shrill than she meant it to be, but the sight of his hands made her feel sick. She tried to push herself to her feet and made it up to sitting before her body failed her. She groaned but glared daggers at Dad when he moved closer to help.

When she looked at him, all she saw was the way he'd picked that woman up and smashed her into the tree. And now he wanted to pick her up with those same hands. Her throat tightened as bile rose higher. She swallowed hard, forcing it down. "Give me a moment."

Dad's lips were tight, and his eyes darted around the trees, but he nodded.

Sascha breathed in deeply, forcing her chest and stomach to expand and contract. She was as good as her word. She found the strength to rise, and though her legs felt weak, she trusted she wouldn't fall.

Dad looked like he wanted to ask a question, but he decided silence was wiser. He stared for a long moment, then turned to lead them north.

Sascha pretended she didn't notice the hurt in his eyes.

THE SCARRED WOLF

Kalen closed his eyes to listen to the whispers of the woods. Birds sang in the west, but to the north, they were silent. He hadn't heard anything from the east since the ambush, either. Their enemies tightened the snare around them, but Sascha's labored breathing prevented him from knowing more. Twice he bit his tongue as he was about to snap at her.

She was a fool, yes, but also young. He'd not trained her for this. The hunting party had singled her out with ease, and if he'd been a little later in recognizing the danger, there was no telling what would have become of her. She hadn't listened, but he blamed himself.

Her broken nose prevented her from breathing easily, and she was still in pain from the beating she'd endured. Finally, her steps fell behind, and he was forced to stop. He turned to see her with her hands on her knees. He wanted to go to her, to help her, but she refused his aid. She wanted nothing to do with him now that she'd seen him truly.

Once she'd caught her breath, she asked, "Why do we need to run?"

"We're being hunted."

Sascha straightened and looked at the trees as though they might attempt their own ambush. "Where?"

"North and east, for sure. Maybe to the south. It's hard for me to tell."

"Then why aren't we heading west?"

"There's no safety that way."

"But there is to the north? Where a hunting party is waiting for us?"

They didn't have time for the conversation. "I can explain soon. For now, we need to run. It's not much farther. Can you use your runes to gain some strength?"

"I'll try."

She closed her eyes and focused, just the way he'd taught her. Then she channeled her will into the rune. She stood taller as the lethargy dropped from her muscles. He grinned. It wasn't easy to focus on one's will when they were tired and bruised.

He did the same, and together they ran.

Kalen didn't know this area, but it hardly mattered. After a lifetime of rune work, he could sense a locus of power nearly a day away. The one in the forest was stronger than most he'd passed through.

But could they reach it before the hunters tightened their snare?

Sascha's renewed vigor gave him hope, but it was slim. His hand itched for the comforting weight of Fang. Instead of pulling it from its sheath, he ran faster, pleased to hear Sascha keeping pace.

His focus narrowed. The hunters were close now, so

much so he could see the shadowy figures paralleling them. He pumped his legs and glanced back to ensure Sascha remained on his heels. More shadows gathered to the south, closing quickly.

He crashed between a handful of thick oaks and into a large clearing. He stopped running, and Sascha almost crashed into his back.

"They're right behind us!" she shouted.

"I know." He took out his water skin and took a sip. "Thirsty?"

She stared at him as though he'd gone mad, and he grinned.

Before she could shout more at him, their pursuers emerged from the woods. They came in twos and threes, all of them glowering like someone had stolen a feast from them. Kalen took a long, slow sip from his skin.

"Dad?" Sascha asked. She backed away from the scorpions until she was almost pressing against him. For the moment, she'd forgotten how much she detested him.

Kalen returned the skin to his pack. "Let's see what we can do about your nose. If we don't have too much company, I'll teach you a rune that will speed the healing."

"Dad!" she gestured at the scorpions.

"They'd be fools to attack us here," he said.

"Why?" she asked, with the doubt he would have expected if he'd claimed the sun would never rise again.

"This is a sanctuary. If they attacked us, they'd be breaking an ancient peace. Not only would their lives be forfeit, but Kunama's as well."

He wished he was as confident as he sounded. A few of the scorpions looked angry enough to risk it. But none could reach him before he could draw Fang, and that was comfort enough.

Sascha looked far from convinced, but she followed him as he looked for a seat. He found a promising spot several hundred paces in. Four small trees had grown roughly into the shapes of chairs, and Kalen settled in one gratefully. He wasn't actually tired, but his pursuers were all much younger, and he saw no harm in persuading them that age had weakened him.

The power here impressed him. He'd visited sanctuaries before, but few refreshed him the way this one did.

Before long, the scorpions melted back into the woods on some unspoken command. Kalen watched them go. Most likely, they would surround the sanctuary, but did they have enough hunters?

He figured it was a question he could answer later. Healing Sascha took precedence over any escape plans.

Sascha sat in another of the chairs, looking very much like she was expecting to wake up from a dream at any moment now. He rose from his chair, walked over, and kneeled before her. He intended to set her nose, but she recoiled as he came close. It was a subtle movement, but it stopped him cold.

He thought of when she had been little, how she had run to him whenever he returned from the fields. Sometimes, those memories felt like they had been days ago. Other times, like today, it felt like it had been an age since she'd expressed any sign of concern or affection.

Her gaze was focused on his hands, still covered in blood. "Sorry. I'll wash them off first."

Kalen sensed the new arrival a moment before he saw Sascha stiffen in surprise.

"If only it was so easy to wash the blood of your sins from your soul," the visitor said.

Kalen had suspected, but hearing the familiar voice laced with anger broke his heart. "Naga. I wondered if that might be you."

He stood and positioned himself far enough to the side Sascha could see but close enough he could prevent Naga from reaching her.

Naga stood as tall as Kalen, but the years had changed him. His hair was lighter than it had been up in the mountains, and he'd lost some of his bulk, but he looked as dangerous as ever. He'd traded in his sword for the longer, thinner blades the scorpions favored, but Kalen suspected he was as skilled with it in his hand as he had been with northern steel.

Naga smirked. "Hid too well?"

Kalen nodded. "I've never known anyone else who could mask their presence so well. And you always were partial to splitting forces. I may not have caught your scent, but the plan reeked of you all the same."

"I'd worried all that time hiding might have made you soft," Naga said.

"It did. Still should have tracked you down."

The smirk slid from Naga's face. "I'll enjoy killing you, old friend."

"It's come to that?"

Naga snarled and snapped his jaw as he stepped face to face with Kalen. "You think it would be otherwise? On the day we needed you most, you weren't there. Our certain victory turned to defeat, all because one of Bonde's bitches had stolen your seed and unmanned you."

Kalen had his hand on Fang before he realized what he

was doing. The blade hummed as he gripped it, eager to breathe again after being buried so long.

But the old laws that restrained Naga's vengeance stilled Kalen's hand as well. Naga's glare dared Kalen, but the taunts weren't quite sharp enough. His friend's eyes narrowed. "You've calmed down. When I knew you, such an insult would have destroyed a camp."

Kalen tilted his head in Sascha's direction. "If nothing else, children teach patience."

"In this, we agree," Naga said. His posture eased, though Kalen suspected he could still have a sword in hand in the blink of an eye. He offered Sascha a shallow bow. "My name is Naga. I'm grateful the gods arranged this meeting."

Sascha glared at Naga and didn't answer.

Kalen returned the bow on his daughter's behalf. "Apologies. This is Sascha, my daughter."

Finally, it was more than Sascha could take. "He's trying to kill us, Dad! Why are we talking with him?"

"Because he's an old friend, and the next time we meet, it's unlikely both of us will live to speak of it."

Kalen took a knee and bowed deeply. "Though it means little now, I apologize for my actions that day and for every day after. Had I known another wolf survived, I would have followed you to the ends of the world."

Naga snarled again. "You are the only wolf here, traitor."

He lifted his shirt to reveal an old scar in the center of his chest. Long ago, he'd been branded over the heart with Kunama's mark.

Though Kalen had suspected as much, he recoiled at the sight of the brand. The list of his sins was long, but despite what Naga believed, he'd never disobeyed any of Vilkas's commands.

"Were you tortured?" He prayed the answer was yes, so he wouldn't think less of his friend.

"Not by the scorpions," Naga said. "There was no need. What could they do? What could they take away from me that you hadn't already? Jolon offered me a purpose and promised to let me hunt you if you ever returned. I bear this mark proudly."

Kalen bowed one last time before rising to his feet, acknowledging his complicity. "Would you stay and eat with us? I was going to teach Sascha Vilkas's healing runes, then break our fast."

"She doesn't know the healing rune?"

"She only recently learned of her heritage. I'd hoped to give her a start in life unburdened of my sins."

"Dad, why are you telling him this?" Sascha said.

"They already know you lack the skill to be a threat. I'm not sharing anything harmful. Now come, and I'll set your nose for you. Naga already knows the rune well."

By the time Kalen had set her nose, taught her the healing rune, and ensured she could use it well enough to heal the remaining wounds, the sky was turning blue.

Sascha wandered a little way away to have some privacy and come to terms with all she'd learned in the night. Kalen sympathized. It was a lot, and he had already thrust her into a world she didn't understand. She was handling it well, all things considered.

"Do you have children, Naga?"

"I do. Three boys who are terrors and one girl too good for this world."

"They change you, don't they?"

"More than I care to admit."

Kalen sat down and rummaged through his pack. He

pulled out some dried meat and passed a piece to Naga, who sat across from him and accepted the offering. They chewed in silence for a while.

Naga spoke first. "There have been days when I hoped you were dead, so I could be free of your memory."

"I'm sorry to have burdened you for so long."

"Was it worth it?"

Kalen looked over to where Sascha was pacing, muttering angrily to herself. "It was, though I'll always wish I had found a different way."

He turned back to Naga. "I would hear of your life, though. You are bonded, and a father. Much has changed since we parted."

Naga obliged, spinning the tale of the last decade and a half. How he'd survived the last hunt of the wolves only to be caught by the scorpion's sting. How a young man named Jolon had earned his loyalty. Naga smiled as he told Kalen of his family.

When he had finished, Kalen returned the favor. He told Naga about his life with Embla and Sascha and about his efforts to make a home in the village. Naga listened closely, his reactions ranging from amusement to confusion.

When Kalen finished his story, Naga asked, "Did you like such a life, stuck in one place?"

"I struggled with it," Kalen acknowledged. "But it has its benefits. Sascha grew up with little fear of violence, and she never knew the suffering of a truly lean winter. Before this, I had hoped she might live peacefully all her days."

Naga considered that then snarled softly. "You lie to yourself, old friend. There is no animal in this world that knows a life of peace. Violence is our fate."

"Perhaps. It was a pleasant lie while it lasted."

Kalen bit off the last of his meat. "We don't need to do this. I don't want to deprive your children of their father."

"I could say the same of you. Turn around with your tail tucked between your legs and return to Bonde. It won't save you, but you may earn a few more seasons of peace."

Naga studied him closely. "You can't, though, can you?" He turned to glance at Sascha. "Vilkas called her, didn't he? That's why you've come out of hiding after all this time."

Kalen saw no point in denying what Naga had already figured out. "He did."

Naga sighed. "Oh, Kalen. You're a damned fool." He stood. "When I kill you, I will make it quick. I'll grant her the same."

Kalen rose, too. He bowed deeply. "It's been a pleasure to see you again. I regret it couldn't have been under happier circumstances."

Naga returned the bow and left the clearing, heading north. Kalen watched him depart, then looked for Sascha. He owed her explanations.

But he couldn't see her anywhere.

DREVA

Sascha wanted to hit something, to break something, to crush something in her palms. She made fists, then stretched her fingers out wide and shook her hands out, only to make tight fists again. Whenever she blinked, she saw the scorpion warrior lifted off her feet and driven headfirst into the tree. By Dad. The man who'd taught her to avoid violence.

He'd never raised a hand against her, though she'd certainly given him plenty of cause over the years.

And he had killed the scorpion without a shred of mercy, without a hint of hesitation.

He couldn't be both killer and father, yet he was. Her thoughts jumped back and forth, trying to weave these disparate threads into a tapestry she could understand. All she ended with was a tangled mess of knots.

Now he broke his fast with the commander who had ordered her death. They greeted each other as old friends. Dad had even chastised her for her poor manners in front of their enemy!

He betrayed her, over and over. First with his lies, then with Naga.

Sascha understood the risk of leaving their sight, but she couldn't stand watching them talking. She could feel the peace of this grove, though, and was reasonably certain she would stay within the sanctuary's bounds.

Truthfully, she was terrified of leaving.

Dad had warned her. Gifted as she was, she lacked the experience and skills needed to survive outside Bonde's lands. Strength and runes alone didn't make a warrior. If she broke whatever strange truce ruled this clearing, she'd pay for it with her life.

She ducked behind a large oak that hid her from her father's sight. It barely counted as hiding, but it let her believe she was alone. She leaned back against the tree, raised her face to the canopy, and sighed.

It was going to be a gorgeous day, but she'd not noticed earlier. The sun broke through the canopy as the breeze pushed the leaves back and forth. The day promised unusual warmth this deep into autumn, but the shade of the trees kept her cool. She closed her eyes and let the sun and leaves cast their patterns of light and shadow across her skin.

When she opened her eyes again, she saw an old woman walking toward her. She frowned, but after the last few days, lacked the will to question anything new. The woman had bright red hair and a smile that shone like the sun. Sascha considered returning to the clearing and the safety of her father's gaze, but she sensed no danger from the visitor.

Still, she'd learned her lesson from the ambush. She didn't know what she didn't know. She pushed off the tree and was about to return to the clearing when the stranger spoke. Her voice was soft. "There's no need to fear, Sascha. No harm will come to you in my home."

"Your home?"

"Yes, dear. One of many, but one of my favorites. Do you like it?"

Sascha looked around. "It's peaceful. It reminds me of a place close to where I lived. A grove near my house."

"That grove is young still, but I'm partial to it as well. Bonde's lands are as good for trees as they are for crops."

Sascha's eyes narrowed. "Are you a god, too?"

The woman smiled, which made Sascha feel more at ease, though she couldn't say why. "Some would say so, but you must forgive my poor manners. My name is Dreva, dear."

Remembering her father's chastisement, Sascha gave a quick bow. "Sascha. It's a pleasure to meet you. Do you live here?"

"Sometimes. But I'd rather ask about you. You looked unsettled when I approached. What's wrong?"

Sascha would have pushed most who asked away, but she couldn't bring herself to treat Dreva that way. For the past several days, she'd seen no one but her father and people who wanted to kill her. And there was something about Dreva that put her at ease. The red-haired woman reminded her, a little, of Sonje. Wise, caring, and ready to listen.

"It's hard to know where to start," Sascha said. "How much do you know?"

"I know everything that's happened to you, but I don't know what's in your heart. Why are you here, instead of beside Kalen?"

"He's sitting next to a man who wants to kill me. They're breaking their fast together like they're old friends."

"They are old friends."

Sascha was about to object, but the old woman took her hand. "Come with me. They won't see us if we remain close to the tree."

Together, they walked around the tree, and just as Dreva had claimed, neither warrior so much as glanced in their direction.

"What do you see?" Dreva asked.

"Dad, sharing our hard-earned supplies with the man who is supposed to kill us."

The answer didn't bother Dreva in the slightest. Sascha wondered if anything could wipe the smile off the woman's face. Dreva said, "Look, Sascha. Really look. Your father confuses you, but the answers are there if you can open your eyes and see him truly."

Sascha sighed, but supposed there was little benefit to arguing with a god. She stared, and as she stared, she clenched her fists tighter. She wanted to snarl but didn't dare draw more attention. Her fingernails dug deep into her palms, but she watched.

In time, her fists relaxed. Dad smiled as Naga spoke, far more than she was used to. He leaned closer to hear every word and nodded often.

This was a side of her father she rarely saw. In the village, he'd been well respected, but he'd always held himself at a distance. Few sought him out unless there was work to be done or a favor asked. There'd been no animosity among their neighbors, but there'd been little affection, either.

"He's trying to kill us," Sascha repeated. "Why is *he* the one Dad speaks so freely to?"

Dreva answered after a brief pause. "You look at Naga and see only a sliver of the man, one bound up in revenge and his twisted sense of honor. It's not that Kalen is ignorant of these facts, but he sees much more. They've shed blood together, and such ties aren't easily abandoned. And it's not as though Naga's vengeance is without reason. Long ago, your father caused his greatest suffering. Many of Naga's closest friends died that day, based on a choice Kalen made."

The god's answer unsettled Sascha. She couldn't remember ever seeing Dad so comfortable. Whenever she and he spoke, he was on edge, as though traversing a battlefield with hidden dangers. She'd witnessed the same with others, though it was rarely as pronounced.

"What happened between them?" she asked.

"That's a story better left for your father to tell. All you have to do is ask."

Sascha had seen enough. She retreated to the other side of the tree. Dreva followed, half walking, half gliding over the grass.

"He never belonged in the village, did he?" Sascha asked.

"Kalen is a wolf, through and through. Vilkas never raised one finer."

"Why did he stay, then?"

She answered her own question. "I know. I should ask him."

Sascha turned her attention to Dreva. "So, why are you here?"

"To speak with your father, and to meet you. Your name is on many lips these days."

She snorted. "Why?"

Dreva's smile was mysterious. Instead of answering, she pointed to the clearing. "They're done."

Sascha poked her head around the corner of the tree and saw that Dreva spoke true. Dad and Naga bowed to one another, and Naga left. Sascha's gaze was drawn to Dad, who looked heartbroken to see his friend depart.

Then he noticed she was missing, and his sorrow turned to panic.

Sascha stepped out before he became worried. He sighed deeply and slumped back down in the strange chair. "You frightened me—"

He caught himself before he said, "girl." Maybe there was hope for him yet.

Dreva emerged from the trees, but Dad's only reaction was to raise an eyebrow. "Dreva. It's good to see you again."

"Likewise. It's been many seasons since our paths crossed."

"Thank you for your protection."

"You're a strange man, Kalen. With one breath, you curse the gods, but with the next, you thank us for our gifts."

"I've no qualm with elders. Only the children squabbling drives me to madness."

"What plan do you have for leaving this place? Naga and his scorpions already have the clearing surrounded."

Dad yawned. "No plan. I was going to sleep on it and see if anything came to me. If not, I'll break through."

"The Kalen I once knew would have fought first and never considered the alternatives."

Dad shrugged. "Would prefer not to draw Fang, if possible."

"I would help you, if you ask."

Dad's eyes narrowed. "For what price?"

"None."

"Nothing comes without a price."

Dreva pointed to Sascha. "I want to see her succeed."

Sascha's heart skipped a beat. Why did the gods care what happened to her?

Dad had the same question. "Why?"

"She's the child of two runemasters, so different they may as well have come from separate worlds. Our gifts flow strong in her blood. Opposing forces find balance in her. One god grows while another fades. One hunts, while the other grows deep roots. We will need her in the days to come."

"I tire of vague words and empty prophecies," Kalen said. "If you and the others see something in Sascha's future, I beg of you to simply speak of your visions."

Dreva stepped closer to Dad and lifted her hand to his cheek. He let no one get that close to him, but he made no effort to push her away or flee. "You hate us so much, but know us so little."

The elder god sounded surprised, but to Sascha, that seemed like it was usually the way of the world. Understanding shattered hate.

Dreva continued, "We can't see the future any more than you, Kalen. But we see what has been, and we know what is. All we do is draw a line from past to present, then extend it into the future."

"And what does that practice tell you about my daughter?"

Sascha leaned forward, eager to hear the answer herself. Lysabel's village had always felt so small to her. Was a greater destiny prepared?

"I know nothing about your daughter that you don't. But you've cut yourself from our realm, so you're no longer aware of our divisions. Bonde is the herald of a new age, and he makes us all nervous. You might think of him as the first of a new generation, one whose yoke is far lighter than those of us who came before. Kunama isn't the only one who would strike him down before he grows into his power. Bonde needs someone to stand for him, and Sascha has the most potential of all his people. That is why she matters."

"So, you want to see Bonde succeed?" Sascha asked.

"I do. Bonde will reshape everything, but he is the one who will bring a new age of prosperity to humanity."

"Why do you care?" Sascha asked.

Dad answered the question for her. "The great secret the gods don't want us to know. They need us as much as we need them. Their power comes from us. If humanity thrives, so do they."

Dreva didn't deny it. "I can offer you safe passage and put you a day or two ahead of Naga."

"How?"

"A true spirit walk to the next sanctuary."

Sascha saw the way her father glanced at her. "What?" she asked.

"What Dreva suggests is a hard path. Humans struggle within the realm of the gods, and it's easy to lose yourself forever," he said.

"What other choice do we have?"

"We walk north, and I fight the scorpions when they attempt to stop us."

"How is that any safer?"

Dad shrugged. "Most of the scorpions don't worry me much. But Naga has considerable skill and has held onto his vengeance for a long time. Our battle would hinge on whether I can kill him."

Sascha thought about her father, sitting across from

Naga, pleased to see his old friend again. She thought of that battle in the woods between him and the scorpions, and she shivered.

He worried that if they took Dreva's path that she might lose herself. But she worried that if they took his, she would lose her father for good.

As angry as he made her most days, she didn't want that.

She turned to Dreva. "We'll accept your generous offer. Thank you."

Dad's face fell, but she also sensed the relief of not having to face Naga yet. She couldn't say she understood Dad's relationship with the scorpion, but her father's emotions were plain to see. He'd never hidden them well.

The decision made, Dad put himself in charge once again. "We'll want to rest and recover before we attempt the journey. How long do you think it will take once we begin?"

"Time has less meaning there, but not long," Dreva replied.

"Do you think you'll feel well enough to travel by this evening?" Dad asked Sascha.

She nodded. Thanks to the runes, her nose and torso were already feeling better. After a full day of sleep, she was certain she'd be up for anything.

By the time evening came, she wasn't so confident about her decision. Dad kept checking his weapons and pack, hiding his nerves behind a mask of constant activity. Dreva had disappeared during the day. Now that night had fallen, she paced the clearing while she waited.

Finally, Dad could delay no longer. He stood, threw his pack over his shoulders, and nodded to Dreva.

The mysterious woman led them out of the clearing and to a giant oak. Dreva gestured, and the bark appeared to melt and twist. It opened wide until it was big enough for Dad to crawl through. Dreva gestured again, and the transformation ended.

Sascha stared into the darkness and shivered. The hole in the tree angled down, and she imagined crawling to the next sanctuary under the ground on hands and knees. No wonder Dad had hesitated about taking this route. But she had resolved to do this, to save Dad from having to fight his friend. If this were the price, she would pay it.

Dreva offered one last caution. "When we enter, you must be cautious and stay close behind me. If I lose you, I'm not sure I'll find you again."

"Find something to focus on," Dad added. "It could be a memory, or a thought, or even the rising and falling of your chest. The other realm is a strange place, but distraction will always be dangerous."

Sascha knew this all already. She'd endured lectures from Dad from the moment she'd woken. But it was good to hear them one more time. His constant reminders slowed the pounding of her heart. His familiar nagging gave her something to focus on.

Dreva dropped to her hands and knees and crawled through the hole in the tree. She didn't gradually fade from sight, the way Sascha would expect. Instead, she was fully visible one moment, then gone the next. Sascha blinked, but Dreva didn't return.

Dad gestured for her to follow. "I'll be right behind you."

She started to sweat. This was it. He was going to leave her. Abandon her to the gods.

She clenched her fists and shook her head, refusing to listen to her fears.

Then she got down on hands and knees and crawled into the realm of the gods.

PASSAGE

Kalen's chest constricted as Sascha disappeared into the tree. He had meant to express his gratitude for her willingness to risk everything for his sake, but now she was gone, with only his warnings to guide her way. Already the tree was closing as Dreva and Sascha journeyed deeper into a realm few mortals touched, so he dropped to hands and knees and crawled through before it sealed shut.

The transition came sooner than he expected. One moment he was inside a tree, and the next he wasn't. Faint green lines illuminated a tunnel that squeezed in on all sides. The bottoms of Sascha's boots were less than the width of a hand in front of his face, and he took comfort in the sight.

"Everybody in?" Dreva asked.

Sascha said, "Yes," and Kalen grunted.

Though the tunnel was large enough for him to crawl on hands and knees and breathe without difficulty, he found it difficult to pull enough air into his lungs. He kept looking up and expecting to see the night sky filled with stars and the watchful eye of the moon. Instead, he bumped the back of his head against the top of the tunnel.

His breaths came fast and shallow. He focused all his attention on Sascha's boots. He was here for her. Nothing would scare him away.

Without warning, Kalen sensed a wave of Dreva's power. The tunnel expanded, swelling to several times its original size. Ahead of Sascha, Dreva stood, glowing faintly with the same green light as the lines above. Though she'd crawled through the same rich soil as Kalen, her clothes were as clean as if they'd just emerged from a mountain spring.

Sascha stood, too. "Where are we?"

"Welcome to the realm of the gods, Sascha. You've visited in your dreams, but this is something deeper. Few mortals have ever walked these paths."

Sascha looked around the tunnel as Kalen carefully stood. He kept expecting the tunnel to constrict again, but there was just enough height for him to stand. Almost as if Dreva had shaped it to be Kalen-sized.

Sascha ran her fingers along the green lines. As Kalen's eyes adjusted, he saw how they bent and wiggled like the roots of a forest's worth of trees. A shiver ran up and down Sascha's spine.

"Incredible," she whispered.

Kalen lifted his hand and touched a root. It was slightly warm to the touch, but otherwise unremarkable.

Sascha, though, was entranced. "They all talk to one another, don't they?"

"Can you hear them?" Dreva asked.

"Faintly, but I don't understand. It's a little like listening to the scorpions when they speak in their own tongue."

Dreva fixed Kalen with a satisfied look, but Kalen didn't understand its meaning.

"Is it all like this?" Sascha asked.

Dreva shook your head. "Think of this like a doorway, an in-between space. The next part will be the most difficult. Are you ready?"

Sascha nodded, but the most Kalen could manage was another grunt. He feared that if he spoke, his voice would crack, and they would know his weakness.

"Stay close behind me," Dreva said. "I will shield you as well as I'm able."

Dreva advanced, and once again, the transition happened in an eye blink. Dreva's dark tunnels vanished, and they were in the woods. Oaks and pines grew shoulder to shoulder, their branches intertwined like lover's arms. The trunks were so close that Kalen had to turn sideways to fit through the gaps, and when he glanced back the way he'd come, even those gaps had vanished. A wall of trees hugging each other tightly blocked his retreat, though he'd heard nothing move.

As the Fang of Vilkas, he'd had the honor of walking in this realm before, though it manifested differently for each of the gods. Vilkas was a god of open skies, rugged mountains, and raging rivers. There, Kalen had felt as at home as he did in the tent he'd carried on his back. The realm had pushed against his presence, but gently, a constant reminder that he didn't belong.

Here, it felt as if every tree had eyes that stared deep into his heart and found him wanting. They permitted him only because he followed Dreva, but even that welcome was tenuous. Gaps seemed to narrow as Sascha passed them, as though the trees were trying to cut him off from his escorts.

When Kalen glanced up, the canopy was so thick he felt as if he were underground again.

He swallowed his fears and shuffled forward faster. Dreva glided around the trees as though being passed from neighbor to neighbor at one of Lysabel's dances. Sascha followed, her presence feeling much the same, even if her steps were less certain. She belonged here in a way Kalen never could.

Then his daughter fell to her knees with a cry. She clutched at her throat as though a rope choked the life from her. Her eyes went wide, and her face turned purple. Kalen ran to her and felt around her neck, but he neither felt nor sensed anything.

He looked around and shouted, "Vilkas!"

"He's not responsible, at least not directly," Dreva said.

She closed her eyes and put her hand on Sascha's shoulder. She shuddered, and the trees surrounding them creaked and groaned as though blown by a powerful summer storm. Kalen looked up as a crack split the air, expecting a tree to fall on them from above.

Nothing fell, though, and he returned his attention to Sascha. He wanted to pound on her back, to shake her, to do anything, but there was nothing useful he could do. It was the most worthless he'd been since the days he was forced to watch Embla waste away from illness.

Not Sascha, though. He couldn't lose her. "Can we get out?" he asked.

Dreva shook her head as another convulsion racked Sascha's body.

Then Sascha took a deep, gasping breath, and some of the color returned to her face. Dreva shouted and was picked off her feet and thrown into one of the trees that surrounded them like guardians. The elder god hit hard, then slid down the side of the trunk.

"Keep her focused," Dreva coughed.

Kalen picked Sascha up. "Sascha, girl. Can you hear me?"

Her eyes fluttered open, and she moaned. Her gaze focused on him for a moment, then past him.

"Sascha!"

Her eyes focused again.

"You need to stay with us. Focus on me." He watched her try, but the pull of this realm was too strong for her.

Dreva found her feet and helped take some of Sascha's weight. The blow she'd taken was strong, but she walked as though unharmed. As soon as Dreva supported Sascha, more of Sascha's awareness returned. She put weight on her feet, easing some of Kalen's and Dreva's burden.

"What's happening?" she asked.

"I'll explain later," Dreva snapped. "For now, we need to leave this place as quickly as possible. Stay with us, Sascha."

Dreva pulled them forward. She stayed under one of Sascha's arms while Kalen hunched over and supported the other. Kalen could track his daughter's focus by how steady her steps were, and it faded quickly.

"Talk to her," Dreva said, noticing the same. "Give her a reason to stay. Tell her a story."

After the events of the past day, one story rose above all the others. And if she didn't remember it when they left the god's realm, so much the better.

"I'll tell you why I left my homeland. Why Naga has waited more than a decade to claim my soul in the hunt."

Sascha's steps steadied. She even found the strength to

speak, albeit slowly, as if pushing out each word was an effort. "Sounds like...ngh... interesting story."

Kalen thought for a moment, choosing the best place to begin. Had he been telling the story around a campfire, he might have found a more meaningful beginning, but Sascha's suffering demanded haste.

"The wolves of Vilkas were always a small clan. Bonde already has many, many times the number of people the wolves had, even at their peak, and I wasn't born in their greatest moment. Life in the northern mountains was always hard, but the clan suffered through many lean years when I was a child. Neighboring clans sensed our weakness, and after years of strife, took advantage."

Sascha stumbled, but Kalen caught her easily. Telling the story gave him something to focus on, a past that still felt far more real than the forest he walked through.

He continued. "All of this is of little importance. I only tell you to give you some idea of how difficult my childhood was. I grew up hungry, watching my clan wither and die before my eyes. As I grew older, though, I discovered my gifts. Runes came naturally to me, and once I'd developed a certain proficiency, Vilkas taught me more. I became the strongest runemaster in the clan by the time I was your age, and I turned that skill towards the hunt, protecting my clan from enemies and filling their bellies with fresh meat."

Trees continued to part before them. Kalen's blood burned and his thoughts turned, not of his own accord, to another tree in a distant land. His throat burned at the memory, but he fought the temptation to let the past consume him.

Sascha needed him now, so he skipped to the most difficult part of his tale. "I could speak for days of those years. Much blood was shed, and I grew both in skill and in honor among my clan. Word of my deeds spread to the neighboring clans. They saw us regaining some of our old strength and feared the battles to come. They banded together to kill the wolves once and for all."

Kalen swallowed the lump in his throat. "This was about the time I met your mother. Scorpions had captured her and her family and they were forced to serve one of their chiefs. Most of her family died in that service, but she and her brother survived. When I killed the chief, I freed them from their bonds. The brother swore himself to the wolves, and Embla was caught between her desire for home and the comfort of her only family.

"Though she made no oaths, we treated her as one of our own. She was a skilled runemaster in her own right, though her skills were as different from mine as night is from day. She healed both plants and animals with a word. I fell in love with her love of life. I'd grown up knowing only the hunt and death. Embla revealed a side of life I'd never experienced before."

Kalen felt the pressure on his thoughts ease. The gaps between the trees grew wider, but he was still grateful they all clung to one another. Dreva may walk these paths with ease, but they would never welcome a mortal's step. Sascha still struggled, but the story kept her present with them.

"Both my love and the threat of the other clans grew that fateful summer. Your mother cared little for me at first, but in time, something changed. I'll never understand what made her return my love, but that summer we were bonded, and the memory of that ceremony remains one of the happiest of my life."

Kalen sighed. "In my own life, all was well. Embla

became pregnant soon after, and my skill and legend grew with every battle. But the clan continued to lose the war. I rarely lost a battle, but I couldn't be everywhere, and our hunting lands shrank by the day. Finally, there came a day when the last battle was near. The opposing clans had gathered together, and the wolves were hungry and afraid. They outnumbered us more than ten to one, and even with my skill, there was no questioning the inevitable."

The trees grew wider yet, and their steps came easier. Even Sascha was probably strong enough now to walk on her own, but they all held onto one another, regardless.

"That night was one of the most difficult of my life. I prayed to Vilkas. I was torn between the honor of my clan that I had given my whole life to and the love I had for my wife and unborn child. I prayed until sweat dripped from my brow, and when I looked up, Vilkas stood before me."

Kalen's throat tightened at the memory of that night. "Vilkas told me to take my wife and unborn child and flee. Even with his permission, it was a hard choice to make. Vilkas told me the remnants of the clan would be destroyed in the next battle. That he wanted me to live. Eventually, he convinced me. I woke Embla, and we fled south."

Ahead of them, an enormous tree towered over all the others. With a gesture, Dreva split the trunk, creating a passage large enough for Kalen to walk through. The passage was darker than a moonless night. They stopped before entering. Dreva took a step apart. "This is as far as I can bring you. Already, my strength grows weak."

Kalen urged Sascha forward. She shuffled forward a few steps before recovering her balance and strength. She vanished into the darkness, but Kalen was only a step behind. Within the tree was much the same as they'd seen before. Green lines of power, shaped like roots, supported the passage. Sascha ran her hand along the walls, and it seemed to Kalen she took strength from the lines. Kalen did the same, but felt nothing.

Sascha vanished from his view, but two steps later, he was through the passage and into another clearing. As before, he could sense the power in this place, and a moment later Dreva emerged from the same gap in the tree that had spit out him and Sascha. The elder god stumbled before Kalen caught her.

When she could stand on her own, Kalen let her go and looked around the clearing. Though it was different, it felt very similar to the one they'd just left. Tall trees surrounded them, but when Kalen glimpsed the sky, he saw that not much time had passed.

"How far did we go?" he asked.

"You're a day, maybe two, ahead of Naga. Be careful as you head north, though. Most paths will take you close to Jolon's winter encampment," Dreva said.

"Thank you. Is there anything we can do for you before we leave?" Kalen asked.

Dreva leaned against a tree. "Make sure she returns to Vilkas. Many of us are counting on her." She gestured for Sascha to approach.

She whispered something into Sascha's ear and traced something on her palm. Sascha whispered, too, and traced something on Dreva's palm. Dreva nodded and smiled, then gave Sascha a gentle push.

Kalen wanted to ask, but Dreva had intended the knowledge only for Sascha. It looked like a rune, but he couldn't be sure.

He was tired, and he suspected Sascha was even more so,

but they couldn't waste a night. Not if Naga remained so close behind. He hoped for some parting advice from her, but she had no words for him. They said their farewells and bowed deeply to Dreva.

When all was done, they fled into the night.

SEEDS OF CHANGE

Sascha thanked the exhaustion that stole the strength from her limbs because it also robbed her of thought. She followed Dad through the night, placing her steps where he'd planted his. When he dropped into a crouch, she did the same. When he ran to take shelter in a copse of trees, she sprinted after him. It was like the games she had played with other children in her village long ago. All she had to do was imitate him. It was easier that way.

Whenever her strength returned, troubling thoughts accompanied them. She was tempted to call them nightmares, but she'd been awake when they first visited.

The passages between the realms had inspired her. She'd never felt as alive as she had when she brushed her hands against the world's roots. Her awareness had expanded beyond the boundaries of her flesh, and she'd felt whole, as though she'd found a part of her she hadn't even realized was missing.

But for as much as she'd welcomed the insights the passages offered, she rejected the gifts of Dreva's realm. That forest had shown her more than she wanted to see. One memory, more vivid than the rest, haunted her when she closed her eyes. A gnarled tree, standing all alone with a jagged mountain peak behind it. She'd never seen the tree before, but the sight sent a shiver down her spine.

Dad's story had pulled her through, keeping her connected to her body as visions overwhelmed her. She'd seen parts of it as he spoke, as though she'd been there in person. She knew, viscerally, about the blood he had shed, the lives he had ended. Visions of his conquests had sickened her.

But the last sight she had seen was that of him, much younger, praying desperately to Vilkas the night before the battle. She'd seen the part before Vilkas arrived and granted him his reprieve, but the longing she'd seen on his face, the torment he experienced as he weighed his responsibility to his clan and his family, she'd never forget.

That was what troubled her most, as they put vast distances behind them. They both used Vilkas's runes, covering more ground in half the night than she would have thought was possible to traverse in two days.

Dad finally called a stop near a stream where the trees grew thick. The sun rose on a new day. She slumped down as Dad started their meal. She rested against a tree and stared at the small stream as it trickled past them. It didn't look like it was wide, even in spring. This late in autumn, it was barely enough for clean water.

Their meal was a collection of late-season berries from Dreva's clearing and dried meat. Back home, Sascha would have complained about the meager feast, but after the long night of travel, it tasted like she was dining with Bonde's eldest chief.

Once her stomach was satiated, she asked, "That story you told in Dreva's realm. It was true?"

Dad nodded, his mouth full of dried meat.

"You left your clan behind to be with us?"

He swallowed. "I did. I didn't want to leave my clan behind, but I couldn't lose you or your mom."

"Do you regret it?"

He looked like he'd swallowed something bitter. "I wish things would have turned out differently or that I'd found another way. But if you put me back in that same position, knowing everything I know today, I'd make the same decision. So no, I don't regret it."

Sascha wished she had known more about Dad when she was younger. He'd always seemed out of place in the village, but she'd also blamed him for not fitting in. If he'd told her about his past, she might have understood.

His silence over the years still made her want to slap him. She wondered what their life would have been like if he'd told the truth about what he'd sacrificed for her.

"I'm sorry that I've been as hard on you as I have," she said.

His smile was brief. "Children are always hard on their parents. There's nothing to forgive."

She wanted to argue, to tell him there was plenty to forgive. She'd been rude and ungrateful. Too often, she focused on what he lacked instead of thinking about what he'd given up for her. But he spoke again, cutting her off before she could make her point.

"It's been a pleasure watching you grow. I see much of both me and Embla within you, but I also see how you have the potential to become much more. Every sacrifice has been worth it."

An icy breeze from the north cut through the trees, and Sascha shivered and wrapped her cloak tighter around her. Dad frowned and sniffed the air. "There's a storm on the way. It's going to get cold soon." His gaze dropped to her cloak. "Is that the heaviest you have?"

A helping of her old anger returned, inflamed by old grievances. How could he not know what she possessed? Not only had she lived her entire life under his roof, but she had packed and unpacked all her supplies in front of him almost every night since they'd left.

She stifled her growl. She understood him better now, but that didn't mean he'd somehow become a perfect father. He could track game for days, but he couldn't keep track of his own boots if they weren't on his feet, much less anything she wore. "Yes, it's my warmest cloak."

"You're going to need something heavier farther north. Might need it as soon as tomorrow night. We'll see."

He seemed content to leave it at that, and Sascha didn't want to pick a fight, so she let the matter drop. She bundled into her hide and fell asleep and was grateful that she was so exhausted that she slumbered throughout the day without dreams.

She woke to the storm Dad had smelled on the air. The wind whipped her blankets around, and the trees creaked and groaned when the wind gusted. Even the calm stream rippled and danced to the wind's demands.

Sascha wrapped her hides tighter and pinned them down with her hands and feet. Dad was already awake, curled up in the lee of a tree with his own hides wrapped tight. The wind blew his unbound hair around, but he didn't seem to mind as the loose strands snapped at his face.

"Get some food in you. As soon as you're ready, we need to leave. It's time to be on the move," he said.

She devoured a quick meal. Movement would warm her frozen limbs faster than huddling deeper under her skins.

They continued north at the same unrelenting pace they'd used the night before, but they didn't make the same progress. This part of Kunama's land was more crowded, and they frequently had to work their way around small camps. When she asked why, Dad said they were nearing Jolon's great camp, where most of the scorpions would eventually settle for the winter.

Sascha guessed they had walked halfway through the night when Dad stopped them. He motioned for her to crouch down beside him. "See the camp up ahead?"

She did. Three tents were nestled in among a small collection of trees as though they could hide from the tempest. Two of the three had smoke drifting from the top, which lasted only a moment before getting caught in the wind.

Heavy flakes of snow fell, whipped about by the gales. One advantage of the storm was that none of the tents had guards posted outside.

"There will be heavier cloaks in those tents. We'll steal one for you."

"Doesn't that risk unwanted attention?"

"It does, so it'll be best not to be seen. I don't think anyone's awake, so you best go now."

"You want *me* to steal one?" she hissed.

"If I do, you'll probably complain I chose the wrong size."

When she glared at him, he chuckled. "I meant it in jest, but yes, you should steal one."

"Why?"

"So I can keep a watch. And because it'll be good for you to learn."

"To steal? You taught me to never steal!"

"Sure, back at home. The rules are different out here. If they didn't want their cloaks stolen, they should have done better guarding them."

Sascha blinked and shook her head. Ever since the night of her spirit walk, it was like she'd woken up to find she had a completely different father. Back home, he'd been very strict about not taking anything that didn't belong to her.

She shook her head again. It wasn't as strange as finding Fang under the floorboards, she supposed. She gulped and nodded. "Any advice?"

His grin was visible even as the wind gusted and blew snow in their faces. "Don't get caught. And don't use your runes. Not this close to Jolon."

She swore and crept forward. When she glanced back, she saw he remained right behind her. She didn't worry about the sound of her footsteps. The howling wind whistling through the trees masked any sound she might make. She reached the first tent long before she was ready.

Sascha almost whispered the runes without thinking. She swallowed hard as she imagined the chief of chiefs riding from his winter camp in response. Calling for Vilkas's help tempted her more than Rolf's sweet-sounding promises ever had, and she wondered what it had been like for Dad, going through all those years without calling on the god he'd relied on for so long.

Another glance reassured her that Dad remained close.

She took a deep breath, then advanced to the door of the first tent. The tent had two rooms. One was many times larger than the other. Sascha guessed it was large enough to sleep somewhere between six and eight people, depending on how close they slept together. The second room was an entryway designed to allow people to enter and leave without disturbing the warmth of the main room.

The flaps of the door had been bound together. If Sascha undid the bottom two knots, she could crawl in, but they had tied the cords on the inside. She argued with herself for a moment, but they'd know they'd be robbed in the morning, so there was no reason to worry about leaving a bit of a trail. She pulled out her knife and cut through the bottom two cords.

The flaps whipped as the wind gusted.

Sascha panicked and rolled to the side. She listened for the sound of a scorpion coming to investigate, but she saw and heard nothing. She held perfectly still until she was convinced the flapping of the doors hadn't bothered anyone within. Then she rolled back to the entrance and crawled through the opening near the bottom of the door.

It felt as though she'd slid into a different world. The winds were muted, and she was warmer than she'd been all night. The bitter wind still brushed against her backside, but it was little more than an inconvenience. She let her eyes adjust to the darkness of the entryway, then stood.

She almost laughed out loud. A pair of heavy cloaks had been folded neatly and left in the entryway's corner. She picked one up and gently unfolded it. It was a little large but was twice as warm as her best cloak. She also figured out why the coat was in the entryway. It smelled like its owner had gotten too close to an angry skunk. She wrinkled her nose, but if the cost of a cloak was a little smell, that was a price she was willing to pay.

Sascha folded the cloak again. She crouched down and put the cloak by the flap so she could crawl out, reach back in, grab it, and be done with the theft. Her movement saved her life. The door to the main room opened, and all Sascha saw was a thin arm holding a knife. It stabbed where her chest had been a moment before.

Then Sascha took a knee to the face, and a weight fell on top of her. She fell back awkwardly, half on her back, half pressed against the knots still holding the flaps together. Something hard drove her down to the ground, and her head and shoulders popped outside the door into the bitter cold.

It shocked her, but something hard hit her in the chest and drove the air from her lungs. She scrambled back, hoping to scrape her assailant off her the way she scraped burnt eggs from the bottom of her pan.

Her assailant wrapped themselves around her torso. Sascha kicked and flopped like a fish out of water and finally escaped the entryway. Her only problem was she'd brought a young woman with her. The sight of a woman about her age, clinging tightly to her waist, stilled Sascha.

The moment of peace gave the scorpion a chance to reposition herself and attack again with the knife. Sascha rolled away from the stab but couldn't escape the grip the scorpion kept on her with her legs. Where was Dad? Hadn't he been right behind her?

The scorpion raised the knife to stab again, but Sascha grabbed the woman's wrist and held on. The woman put her full weight on top of the knife. Slowly but inexorably, the tip of the knife fought its way toward Sascha's chest. Sascha strained, but she wasn't strong enough. She thought of using the runes, but she couldn't shift her focus away from the knife.

The woman hissed and lifted her weight, preparing to slam it down against the knife and finish the deed. At that moment, Sascha twisted and heaved with her hips. The two rolled in the snow. There was a brief time when Sascha felt she had the better position. She was on top of the scorpion, and the knife was under control.

Then neither was true, and Sascha wasn't quite sure what had happened. The scorpion rolled and fell on top of Sascha again. She stabbed the knife down at Sascha's eye. Sascha moved her head, and the knife drew a line of blood down her cheek.

More by instinct than plan, Sascha made a fist. She'd aimed for the scorpion's nose but hit her in the throat. The other woman choked and let go of the knife embedded in the dirt next to Sascha's ear.

Sascha reached behind the woman's head with both hands and pulled her close. She slammed the woman's nose against her forehead and immediately regretted the idea. The scorpion's nose broke, but stars danced in Sascha's vision. They fell apart, each with their heads in hand.

Sascha recovered first. She grabbed the knife in the ground. She had her opening.

The scorpion looked up and met Sascha's gaze as though daring her. All Sascha had to do was stab the woman. She saw the point she'd aim for, right where the knife would slide between the ribs and into the heart.

She couldn't do it. The woman was only protecting her home.

The scorpion lunged at her, but before the woman could

wrap her outstretched hands around Sascha's neck, a shadow materialized behind her. A thick arm coiled around the scorpion's neck, and her eyes went wide. She kicked at the ground and scratched at the arm, but she might as well have been clawing at stone. Before long, she was still.

"Drag her back into the entrance and use these to tie the flaps shut," Dad said as he held a pair of cords out.

Sascha frowned and took the cords, still not quite coming to terms with the fight and its aftermath.

"She's not dead, but she will be if we leave her out here," Dad explained.

Sascha felt her control slipping, but she nodded. She grabbed the woman under the armpits and pulled her toward the tent. Getting the woman in wasn't easy, but enough pushing and pulling got her in well enough. Then she grabbed the new cloak and tied the flaps tight again.

Dad said nothing else. Sascha slipped on the new cloak, grateful for the warmth that spread through her limbs, and they continued their flight north.

NEW HUNT

The wind whipped at Kalen's cloak as he and Sascha lay near the edge of the overhang. Below them, spread out almost like the stars in the sky above, were dozens of small campfires burning bright against the early darkness of autumn. As the sun was setting, they'd crossed paths with a group of slaves carrying wood from the forest down to the camp. Enough wood to build this many fires for a fortnight.

"There's so many," Sascha said.

Kalen had been thinking the same. After the battle in which he'd killed Revon, he'd assumed the scorpions wouldn't last long as a clan. One of the other neighboring clans should have swept in and cleaned up, absorbing the last of the survivors into their own families. Instead, the scorpions had grown since that fateful day. If, as he assumed, many hunting parties still harried the neighboring clans near the borders, the clan was at least twice as strong as they'd been when he fought them last.

Kalen didn't know Jolon, but the feat impressed him.

Only a leader of incredible will could have achieved so much in so little time.

He pointed to the perimeter of the camp. "Notice how each family posts a guard and how the main ways into the camp all have entire hunting parties watching?"

Sascha nodded. "They will welcome no strangers, will they?"

"It doesn't look that way."

"You were thinking about going down there, weren't you?"

"Not seriously," Kalen said, uncomfortable that she'd seen through him so easily, "but I thought that if Jolon died, the most dangerous threat against your life would be gone. Couldn't deny the temptation."

"Is that always how you used to solve your problems?"

Kalen bit back his retort. She'd been on edge since the battle with the scorpion a few nights ago. At first, she'd been furious that he'd let her fight the battle on her own. She hated both that he had tested her, and that she'd failed.

He answered her honestly. "It was, more often than not. Some problems can't be argued with, can't be solved by a bit of extra thought. Some problems need killing. My trouble was I started turning to killing first before trying any of the other ways."

He didn't watch her, but he imagined her scrunching up her face and moving away from him.

"Ready to leave?" he asked.

"Soon." Her stare was locked on the tents below. "So, if this is their winter camp, then come summer, this won't be here?"

"Some might stay, but not many. Come summer, the game in the area will be hunted clean, and the river won't have many fish. War parties will return to the borders and claim more land as their own. For now, they'll rest. Winter is a time for different families to mingle, a time for strangers to fall in love and be bonded. There are a lot of autumn babies, so parents will focus their attention on the new babes. It's a pattern as old as time."

"Seems like too much work."

Kalen chuckled. "I'd say the same about breaking my back in the fields every day trying to raise crops. Hunting can be difficult, but after a successful hunt, there's little to do but sit around for a few days and enjoy the meat. And you get to see so much more of the world."

"You miss it, don't you?"

"There are days. Others, not so much. Someday, you'll realize there is no perfect world. There's only this moment, and it's as good as you make it."

She sighed. "I'm ready to leave now."

They crawled away, putting the ridge between them and Jolon's winter camp. The air was noticeably colder this far north, the mountains not that much farther away. Before long, they would be in territory Kalen remembered from his younger days.

He led the way, careful not to use any of Vilkas's runes. The strongest runemasters would surround Jolon, and they'd be most sensitive to the invocation of a foreign god. They plodded north in the night, their cloaks wrapped tightly around them.

Sascha continued to impress. She'd taken to the hardships of the trail with relative ease, and she kept pace with his long strides with little difficulty. She'd lost a little of the weight she carried back home, and she seemed to enjoy the nip of cold air on her cheeks.

He'd always hoped that she would grow up to be more like her mother, but when he saw himself reflected in her actions and abilities, he couldn't help but feel warm inside. She'd always been capable, and if she survived her initiation, there was no telling what she'd accomplish.

But first, they had to get there, and there was still so much she needed to learn. They had yet to see any sign of Naga or their pursuit, but the hunting party couldn't be far behind.

They fell into a familiar routine as they walked. Kalen taught her what he could of Vilkas's runes. She now possessed a solid grasp of the primal characters. What was more complicated was teaching her how the runes could interact with one another. Between the runes and the power of human will, a creative runemaster's possibilities were endless. But danger lurked around hidden corners. There was a way to the world that not even the gods could break. There were many legends of runemasters attempting impossible feats only to find their runes turning on them.

Runes were some combination of knowledge and inspiration. Kalen could share the vast knowledge he'd built up, but it would be up to Sascha to make it her own.

Two days away from Jolon's camp, Kalen felt safe enough for her to practice the runes again. The first task he set for her was to hunt for their meal for the morning. He understood why she'd hesitated to kill the scorpion. He didn't even blame her. The scorpion had done nothing wrong, and leaving her alive meant the pursuit wouldn't be as fierce.

But the time would come when she needed to kill.

She glared at him when he set the task, but he'd become

inured to her glares the past few weeks. "What do you want me to hunt?"

"Whatever you want, but at least a hare. Enough meat for both of us."

She looked about to argue, but then she stomped off. She knew exactly why he set her on this task.

He followed a ways back, observing how she went about it. With another student, he might have offered more help, but Sascha preferred to find her own way, even if it took her longer. Kalen appreciated her approach. Learning only took root when the student sought the knowledge themselves.

Sascha used runes to hide from sight and mask her scent. Another combination sharpened her senses, and she looked for sign. Kalen let her follow the sign wherever they led, but if they turned south for too long, he suggested finding new prey. Essential as these skills were, they couldn't spare too much time backtracking or walking in circles. Danger lurked too close.

Kalen knew Sascha was a fine shot with her bow. It was the one hunting skill Embla had agreed to let him teach the girl, and she'd taken to it quickly. But she'd never shot at anything that wasn't a target Kalen had put up. The question wasn't if she could hit what she aimed at, but if she'd release the string at all.

Twice that night, they came within bow range of a hare. The first time, Sascha hesitated, and the hare spooked. The second time she hurried too fast, and the hare heard the clack of the arrow against her bow. It, too, darted away before she could shoot.

When the sun dawned that morning, they gave up their hunt and ate some of the provisions remaining in their packs. Kalen said nothing about the failure. Sascha made it clear she would not welcome his comments. He suspected there was nothing he could tell her she wasn't already shouting at herself. It took her much longer than usual to fall asleep.

Kalen's own sleep was fitful. He woke to the passage of several hunting parties close to where they slumbered. Jolon's winter camp was filling, and the numbers terrified Kalen. He couldn't help but imagine the whole scorpion clan after Sascha. No matter her gifts, a single person couldn't fight a clan.

Not for the first time, he wished he could summon Vilkas and take him to task. The old man liked to act like he had some grand plan, but Kalen had never seen a hint. He couldn't believe Vilkas had planned for the destruction of his clan, just like he couldn't believe Vilkas intended to use Sascha's service wisely. The old man was no better than a dying king, grasping at whatever last power remained to him.

He understood Naga well. Maybe it was better for him to kill Vilkas and pray for Kunama's mercy.

He scoffed at his own idea. Kunama had no mercy and never had. If he killed Vilkas, Jolon would thank him for the favor, then kill him and Sascha all the same.

That, maybe more than anything else, was what stoked his anger most. Vilkas hadn't given him a choice. Terrible as the sins of his past were, at least they were his. As Vilkas's Fang, he'd always felt like his thoughts and opinions had mattered.

Now, to keep his daughter alive, he had no choice but to drag her through a war that wasn't her own, to a destiny she'd never have freely chosen.

He swore and clenched his fist.

When he and Vilkas met again, there would be a reckoning.

That night they were up again, Sascha's task the same as the night before. Kalen looked behind them often. Tracking and hunting covered far less ground than their straight march north, and he feared they would have to abandon the hunt soon. But Sascha needed the confidence of a successful hunt. Kalen had already formed plans for his and Naga's next meeting, but they all required support from an archer.

They found tracks not long after they began. Kalen squashed his concerns and let his daughter hunt. Tonight she was already better than last night. She stepped carefully and read the hare's sign well. Before long, she'd advanced into bow range. This time, she displayed none of the hesitation of her first attempt and none of the hurry of her second. She pulled the bowstring back to her cheek, whispered a rune, then released.

As soon as she released, Kalen knew. The arrow flew true, taking the hare cleanly. It was dead before it even knew it had been in danger.

Sascha turned, a wide grin on her face. It was the purest expression of joy he'd seen on her face since back in the village, and it warmed his heart. He returned the smile and bowed. "A perfect shot."

They recovered the hare and resumed their journey north. Kalen felt like there was a spring in his daughter's step that hadn't been there before.

The conversation that night was one of the best he'd ever enjoyed with his daughter. She had questions about how she'd used the runes, and for once, welcomed his advice and suggestions. They talked until the moon was high in the sky. It was the closest he'd felt to her in years.

He didn't say so, though. Even mentioning his contentment risked spoiling the moment.

The sun chased the moon away too soon that night, but they celebrated with a small fire to cook the hare over. Kalen showed Sascha how.

He didn't know how many hares he'd eaten in his life, but the one that night was the tastiest of them all.

He fell asleep easy that day, happier than he'd been since the day Embla fell ill.

That night, he woke to the sight of a hunting party, far in the distance, traveling north.

Naga had finally found them.

ULTIMATUM

Naga slept, but his feet walked the realm of his master. He found himself inside a tent this time, one he recognized as Master's. He stepped inside, kneeled, and pressed his forehead against the floor. Master was there, filling the tent with his presence.

"What news?" Master asked.

"He has passed your winter camp, Master. From his tracks, we believe we are no more than a day behind him. We'll reach him either this night or the next."

Master waited for him to finish, but as soon as he had, he was on his feet. His presence seemed to fill the tent. "He was here!"

Naga felt Master's rage as something physical, like he was being pressed against the walls of the tent. He couldn't expand his lungs to draw a breath, but there was nothing he could do to fight. He would die here if Master wished, and there was no justification for his failure. Master was well within his rights. Naga had allowed the Master's greatest threat to approach too close.

The anger soon passed, and Naga could breathe again. Though Master made no move toward him, Naga knew the edge of a knife was at his throat. The knife wouldn't be satisfied with only his blood, though. It would drink the blood of every member of the hunting party and every member of Naga's family.

"How did this come to pass?" Master demanded.

"Dreva aided them, Master. She provided passage from one of her sanctuaries to another, giving them several days of advantage. Kalen has pressed hard, too."

Naga bowed, ready for Master to end his life.

Instead, Master laughed bitterly. "So, even the elders are against Kunama now. I always suspected this day would come, but I didn't know it would come so soon."

Naga decided silence was the safest course of action.

"Kill him, Naga. Bring his head to me by the full moon, or I will consider your task a failure. Do you understand?"

Naga gulped. "I do, Master."

He woke a moment later in a cold sweat. His feet and legs ached from the chase. Even the youngest and strongest of his warriors had felt the exhaustion of the hunt. When they'd realized what Dreva had done, they'd pulled out their maps. Knowing Kalen would head north, there were only two sanctuaries that made sense. Naga had chosen the one farthest from Master's camp. He assumed Kalen would want to stay as far away as possible, despite Master's beliefs about the old wolf's intent.

He'd chosen wrong, and they'd lost another day or two. The theft of a cloak had set them finally on the right track.

Naga debated between hunting more tonight but decided against it. They needed strength for the battle to come.

He closed his eyes and let his nightmares take him until the morning sunrise.

He told the party of his conversation with Master when they broke their fast the next morning. After, there was no need for him to push them harder. Whatever exhaustion they suffered from was nothing compared to the pain Master would visit upon them if they failed.

Naga appreciated Master's clarity. With his left hand, he rewarded those who were faithful and exceeded his expectations. With his right, he punished those who failed or disobeyed. Serving the master led to the elimination of all doubts. He lived to serve, and his service was richly rewarded. After his last battle as a wolf of Vilkas, he'd expected nothing. At best, he believed he would live out the rest of his days as a wanderer, avoiding any of the clans that sought to kill the last of the wolves. Never would he have thought he would bond with a strong and beautiful woman, a warrior in her own right. Never would he have believed he would raise sons and daughters worthy of Kunama's deepest secrets.

And yet, he enjoyed all of that and more, thanks to Master.

Around midmorning, Zaya joined him. She was his best tracker and the reason they'd rediscovered Kalen's trail as soon as they had. "They aren't much more than a day ahead of us," she said.

"Can we catch them before they leave again?" Kalen and Sascha traveled at night to keep out of sight. Naga chased them during the day. They could cover more ground, and they had nothing to fear from the hunting parties returning to winter camp.

"Maybe not today, but almost certainly tomorrow."

The conclusion didn't come as a surprise, but something must have shown on Naga's face. Zaya, who missed nothing, asked him what was wrong.

"I've waited many years for this. It is still hard to believe the moment is almost here."

"He is an old friend of yours. I observed your interactions when you last met. Will you be able to kill him?"

Naga wouldn't have accepted such a question from anyone else, but Zaya had known him from his earliest days among the scorpions and was the closest thing he had to a friend in the party. They walked apart from the others so that no one else could hear. No doubt, it was a question shared by the rest of the party. By the gods, it was one he'd asked of himself.

"Seeing him again didn't go as I expected," Naga confessed. He glanced around to ensure no one could hear. "I'll not deny that even after everything, there's a part of me that was glad to see him again. Once, he was almost as close to me as my family is today."

Naga thought for a bit, weighing his different feelings. "But seeing him again reminded me that he was never punished for his betrayal. Even if Master hadn't given me the opportunity, I might have hunted him to the ends of the world. He built his life on lies, acting as though he is a man of peace."

"No man of peace could do what he did to our party," Zaya agreed.

"So yes, I will kill him, but when I do, it will be as his friend," Naga concluded.

Zaya bit her lower lip but didn't hide her thoughts from him. "If you would like, we would share this burden with you."

"You already do, just not as you imagine. You know I have nothing but respect for your skills, but Kalen will not be so easy to kill. Without me, I do not think the rest of the party would succeed. Regardless, Master would be displeased."

"All hunt, or none survive," Zaya said.

Naga nodded. "All hunt, or none survive." One of Master's commands, etched upon the heart of every warrior of Kunama.

"What would you have of me?" Zaya asked.

"Continue serving as you have. When the time comes, all of us will bring this hunt to its end. Then we can return to winter camp, and you can begin your hunt for someone to bond with."

Zaya grinned at the thought. She had been bonded once before, but her husband had been a warrior in a party that had retreated before an invasion of foxes to the west. Master had put him and the other cowards to death upon their return, and now Zaya hunted for someone strong enough for her to bond with.

She gave him a slight bow, then ran forward to continue tracking Kalen and his daughter.

It did not go how any of them expected. The pair's tracks roamed east and west, a departure from their normal northward journey. Eventually, Zaya found blood and other tracks and figured out what had happened. She frowned when Naga asked her. "I think he's teaching her how to hunt."

On the surface, such a decision made little sense, but

Kalen did nothing without reason. Naga remembered what had happened to the group he'd used to lure Sascha away from Kalen before. Their deaths had been brutal, and none of them had been at Sascha's hand.

Kalen was once again putting lie to his claim that he was a peaceful man. He knew what tracked him, and he was teaching Sascha to help.

"How was it done?" Naga asked Zaya.

"Bow. An excellent shot, too."

Kalen's decision made even more sense now. He'd been competent enough with a bow in hand, but he was better with Fang up close.

Naga spoke loudly enough for all to hear. "We'll need to be careful as we proceed tomorrow. I suspect we'll face both an archer and a swordsman."

They resumed the chase, but Zaya stopped them early. "They didn't make it as far yesterday. We should camp soon and get some extra rest. We'll meet them tomorrow."

Naga considered the advice and found it good. "Very well. Find a suitable spot, and we'll rest for the evening."

The next day, they made good time, and they found Kalen and Sascha just as the sun began to set.

A WARRIOR BORN

Sascha's breaths were even and her mind calm as they raced through the woods. Tall pines surrounded them, filling Sascha's nose with their pleasant, earthy scent. In one of their spare moments, when they'd stopped so Dad could plan their next steps, he'd mentioned that this was the start of the second great wood in Kunama land.

If they survived the night, these woods would surround them until they were nearly at Kunama's northern border. Though they had plenty of traveling ahead of them, for the first time, Sascha could imagine the end of their journey.

Her biggest problem was that she didn't know what awaited them at the end. Dad had been vague on that point, so much so that Sascha feared the border almost as much as she did the scorpions.

Tonight, though, the scorpions consumed her attention. Since the moment they'd crossed into Kunama land, Dad had kept a pace that would have killed any person or horse. Only Vilkas's runes kept them strong and healthy.

The scorpions had still caught them.

Before they'd entered the forest, Dad had counted seventeen warriors pursuing them.

Dad wasn't as concerned about the number as Sascha thought he should be. Once he'd gotten the count, they'd run north, not much faster than they would have traveled otherwise.

"You're not trying to outrun them?" she asked.

"Alone, maybe. Can't with you."

On any other day she would have been offended, but she was starting to understand Dad had only shown her a fraction of his strength. "So, what are we doing?"

"Finding the best place to fight. And tiring them out some more. I'm surprised at their pace, but they've no doubt been tracking us all day already. We're better rested."

Having more sleep hardly seemed like the decisive edge Sascha desired. She wanted her own hunting party.

It was hard for Sascha to tell how much time had passed as they ran underneath the thick canopy, but she was sure less than half the night had passed when Dad stopped. The trees here were thick, and a steep hill rose sharply to the west.

"This is the place," he said.

Before she could ask, he pointed to the hill. "Climb up that high enough that your position is hard to reach, but low enough you have clear lines of sight to this area. Do you understand?"

Sascha nodded and turned to leave.

Dad grabbed her wrist. "Sascha, do you understand? Kill any scorpions as soon as you have a clear shot. If you don't, they'll certainly kill you."

Sascha's nose ached at the memory of the scorpion's boot breaking it. She knew she'd been fortunate that night. She nodded again.

"I love you, girl," Dad said. "Stay safe."

As she started the climb up the hill, he called after her. "You might not see me, but the battle will be right where I'm standing. You can be certain of it."

She kept climbing. The slope had eroded under heavy rains, and her hands and feet kept slipping. For every two paces she climbed, she slid down one. Exposed roots and stone provided tiny holds, though, and she eventually found a place behind a tree that met Dad's requirements.

Before long, she had the bow strung and most of her arrows within easy reach. She nocked one and took a deep breath. None of this seemed real. She imagined one of the scorpions entering the clearing. She would draw her bow and fire, and just like that, another life would be snuffed out.

Her hands shook, and she wiped her palms, one at a time, against her legs. When the scorpions had humiliated her earlier, she'd been furious enough to kill, but she couldn't find that anger anymore. They hunted her, but some part of her still believed they could reach an agreement.

The sight of Dad preparing for battle steadied her nerves. He had his knife in hand and was carving runes on the north side of many of the trees, where the scorpions wouldn't see them. She couldn't guess what he had planned, but his calm activity grounded her.

Then he turned and gestured to her, making the sign of a rune in the air. She understood. It took her a while to find her center, but once she did, she spoke the first rune he'd ever taught her. Once again, she felt as though it had wrapped her in a warm blanket. She was no longer foolish enough to believe it made her impossible to spot, but it would be harder. With luck, she could take down one or two before they knew where she was.

She shook her head at the thought. The words sounded like they'd come from someone else.

Sascha looked down at her father, but he was gone. She suspected the only one who could find him now was Naga.

Before long, the first of the scorpions stepped into sight. She was moving quickly, her gaze on the ground. Sascha had seen this one before. The woman was older than most in the hunting party but was always in the lead. Most likely, she was the one most responsible for tracking them.

Moving slowly, Sascha raised the bow, and when a breeze rustled the tops of the trees, she pulled back the string.

The woman stopped and stood straight, her hand going to the sword at her hip. She looked around slowly, but she'd stopped in a place where Sascha could hit her easily.

Sascha hesitated, and the tip of the arrow wobbled.

This was different than killing a hare.

She wasn't a killer, no matter how Dad tried to mold her into one.

The woman drew her sword and gripped it in both hands, turning slowly. Sascha was certain she hadn't made a sound, but somehow this woman knew. She was dangerous, the same way Dad was.

And where was Dad? He said the battle would happen here, so why hadn't he attacked? Was this another of his damn tests?

The woman completed a full circle, then stopped and looked right at Sascha.

A small, triumphant smile flashed across her face, and Sascha saw death in that look.

The point of her arrow steadied. She whispered, the rune a prayer for Vilkas's guidance. The arrow came back farther as the strength of her pull increased. She released.

Though the woman was staring at her, something about Sascha's attack caught her by surprise. Perhaps it was that Sascha had fired at all, or perhaps it was the speed and accuracy of the arrow. The scorpion slapped at the arrow with the flat of her blade, but her deflection passed just behind the arrow.

The shot caught her in the chest. She looked down with wide eyes and turned. Sascha saw the tip of the arrow had punched clean through her back. The woman fell to her knees. Sascha held her breath, and eventually, the woman collapsed to her side, never to stir again.

The forest went still. Somewhere in the distance, an owl hooted into the night.

Sascha had killed, and the world didn't give a damn.

But it gave her plenty of time to stare at what she had done. Her hands trembled, but they picked up the next arrow and nocked it without too much trouble.

After it felt like most of the night had passed, more shadows moved through the trees. They slowed and pressed themselves against trunks when they saw the dead woman.

Sascha had no clear shots, a fact for which she was grateful. She focused on her breathing and on keeping her center. Her next shots wouldn't be so easy.

There was more movement in the trees to the south, but it was dark enough and far enough away that she couldn't see well. She whispered another rune, careful not to let the trickle of will that kept her hidden from ending. Her vision sharped in time to see three bodies slump to the ground together. For two, she couldn't see the cause of death, but the last had a second smile carved deep across his throat.

Dad had killed them without a sound.

Once again, stillness fell over the forest. When Dad whispered in her ear, she nearly jumped out of her skin. She'd neither seen nor heard any hint of his approach.

"How are you?" he asked.

She knew the meaning of the question. Could she keep killing for him? Her nostrils flared, but she nodded.

"That was the last of the scouts. The main party will be here soon. I'll draw them to where I was before. Once the battle begins, expect chaos. Take clear shots, but pay close attention to the hill before you. Some may try to climb it while covered in unsight. They'll be easy to miss with the battle raging below."

He reached out to touch her, but when he saw the blood on his hand, he stopped. He bowed instead. "We'll get through this, and then there will be nothing between us and Vilkas."

It was supposed to be reassuring, but it didn't work on her.

She nodded again, just wanting him to leave. She understood what needed to be done.

"See you soon."

Then he was gone, not leaving so much as a trace of his scent on the wind. She searched for some sign of his passage but found none. He was like a ghost that only rejoined the world to destroy it.

She focused her eyes on a spot where there were no bodies and let her attention follow her breath. Once again, she felt as though she had waited for an entire night before she saw more movement. This time, the forest crawled with shadows. Thirteen, if their earlier count had been true.

Dad's voice boomed through the trees. It sounded like it came from all directions at once. "There's still time to avoid this, old friend. I have no desire to kill the last of my pack."

A familiar figure separated from one of the trees. "Then bow your head and allow me to cut it from your shoulders. I will give both you and your daughter a quick and painless death."

Dad appeared down the hill and far to Sascha's left. "You know I cannot submit to such a request."

"Nor I yours," Naga said. He drew his sword, which glowed with the dim light of runes etched upon its blade.

Sascha's heart skipped a beat. Naga had a runed sword, perhaps as powerful as Fang. She'd known, from the way Dad spoke about him, that Naga was dangerous, but that glowing weapon made the statement more clearly than any warning.

Dad didn't draw his sword. He held his hands out wide, but his look wasn't as open and friendly as the gesture implied. "Then let's end this," he said.

Both men vanished, and Sascha swore to herself. She doubted she'd be able to find them unless they wished it, but they weren't the only combatants on the field.

The shadows grew more distinct as the rest of Naga's party advanced. They moved carefully, eyes questing for Sascha's hiding place.

Sascha was about to loose her next arrow when one of the party suddenly collapsed. She frowned. She saw no arrow nor any wound. But to her sharpened vision, it didn't look like the young man was breathing, either.

Before she could answer why, the world fell into the chaos Dad had predicted.

To the south of the party, two trees cracked and fell, blocking the party's escape. Dad appeared as the trees landed, cutting at the party with his knife. Three died before they realized the danger they were in.

"It's a trap!" one yelled, right before Dad drove the tip of his knife through the man's eye.

Naga appeared a moment later, his glowing sword carving ghostly arcs through the air. In the press of bodies, Sascha had no idea how he avoided cutting his allies, but his blade sought only one man.

The battle moved north, and Sascha saw some runes Dad had carved in the trees glow as the scorpions approached.

The sight reminded her that Dad didn't fight alone. She found a scorpion dancing from foot to foot behind Dad, waiting for a moment to strike. Sascha drew her arrow back, whispered for Vilkas's blessing, then released.

Once again, her aim was true, and the scorpion died as the arrowhead sliced through her heart. The death went unnoticed; the scorpions all focused on Dad.

The runes in the trees glowed even brighter. Sascha closed her eyes to block out the light a moment before the runes exploded. Old trees fell upon the combatants, crushing the party as they were forced to choose between the falling trees and Dad's flashing knife.

Dad ignored the trees, dashing among the party with killing blows. None save Naga put up the slightest defense.

As the dust settled, Sascha saw three scorpions had reached the base of the hill. Their eyes were on the battle, their backs to her. She'd never have an easier shot. She nocked an arrow, pulled, aimed, and released in one smooth motion. This time, she didn't even bother calling for Vilkas.

Her arrow caught a scorpion in the back, and the other two turned and looked up the hill. They didn't see her at first, but then she saw one's eyes go wide. He raced up the hill, his feet sliding on the loose dirt. She tried to nock an arrow but missed the bowstring. Her second attempt was more successful, and she pulled back on the string.

She called for Vilkas, and her aim steadied. The scorpion was only halfway up the hill when Sascha released the arrow.

This close, and on hands and knees, the scorpion stood no chance. The arrow went through his eye. He went down hard, snapping the arrow in two against the ground as he fell. Sascha saw, but her attention was already traveling toward the last scorpion.

This one had been slower to react but was quicker on her feet. She was already as far up the hill as her fallen warrior and climbing fast.

Sascha noted the facts but didn't feel the reaction in her body. Her heartbeat was steady and her breaths even. She fitted another arrow to the string and took aim. The scorpion was only two steps away when Sascha released. The arrow barely cleared the bow before it punched into the woman's chest.

Sascha calmly fitted another arrow as the woman looked down in disbelief. She looked back up at Sascha, who waited to see if another arrow would be required. Then she dropped to her knees, lost her balance, and tumbled back down the hill.

Sascha spotted another scorpion near the heart of the battle. Still deep in Vilkas's embrace, she pulled the string back, aimed, and released. The scorpion fell on top of one of the downed tree trunks and didn't move again.

That was enough to earn Naga's notice. Even with unsight covering her, he spotted her without a problem. He left Dad to two of the younger scorpions as he sprinted up the hill.

She had another arrow ready, but when she fired, he slapped it away with his sword. She saw her death in his eyes, but her shot caused him to lose a step, and then Dad was there, cutting at Naga's side with his knife. Naga evaded the cuts easily, dancing backward and down the steep slope as though it were a wide and flat plain.

Sascha grabbed another arrow. She only had three left, so they'd need to be spent wisely. But as she searched for other scorpions, she realized there were none. A few hadn't yet let their spirits free, but they couldn't affect the fight, either. Her gaze jumped from body to body, several with arrows jutting from them. She'd never seen so many bodies before. It didn't bother her the way she thought it should.

Dad and Naga battled in the forest, and it was like nothing Sascha had ever seen before. They were both impossibly quick, many of their strikes so fast Sascha couldn't even follow them. They darted back and forth, searching for the opening that would end the fight. Sascha tried to get a clear shot at Naga, but both warriors moved too fast. She didn't dare waste one of her precious arrows, or risk hitting her father.

Sascha slowly released the tension from the string, waiting for an opportunity. Until then, she watched.

It didn't take her long to realize what was happening. The difference between the two warriors wasn't great, but it was enough, and it was consistent.

Dad was losing the fight.

A WOLF'S END

Kalen leaped at Naga, his knife cutting intricate patterns in the air between them. All he needed was Naga to make one mistake, and this fight would be over. Kalen had once been far stronger, but his time among Bonde's people had weakened him and dulled his edge. Naga had fought hard and grown stronger while he'd bent his back to the work of the fields.

Unfortunately, the closeness of the battle cut both ways. Kalen's first mistake would also be his last. After their meeting in Dreva's sanctuary, Kalen had hoped he could plant a seed of doubt and uncertainty in Naga's burning desire for vengeance. His efforts had failed. Naga's cuts betrayed no hesitation.

Kalen jumped back as his latest attempt failed to break Naga's defenses. He landed on one of the fallen trees and jumped back again as Naga sought to cut him down at his ankles. He'd also hoped the unusual terrain would advantage his knife. The plan had worked well enough against the rest of the party, but Naga adjusted to the shifting battlefield with ease.

Kalen shouldn't have been surprised. Adaptation was the key to survival, and Naga had survived longer than any other wolf.

Naga leaped over the same tree and cut at Kalen. His sword was beautiful in the moonlight. Kalen recognized almost half the runes on the sword, once given to the wolves by Vilkas. The other half lacked the flowing grace of Vilkas's runes. They were jagged and sharp, much like the god who had gifted them.

Kalen couldn't block or deflect that sword with the knife in his hand. He danced backward and around a tree, hoping against hope Naga would miss a step.

Naga didn't, and again he forced Kalen to retreat.

Kalen hadn't expected the fight to be this close. If it continued like this, the victor would be the one who maintained their focus the longest. Once, Kalen wouldn't have doubted his victory in such a competition. Today he wasn't so sure. He had several years on Naga, and the difference in their recent experiences was telling, too.

Naga wedged a toe under a loose branch and snapped it at Kalen's head. He ducked under, but Naga used the moment to pounce. Kalen escaped, but not by much.

Naga paused his pursuit. Kalen hoped Sascha might have an arrow to put through him, but then he saw Naga had stopped in a place where a tree was between him and Sascha. Despite their circumstances, Kalen grinned. "You've improved much since we last fought."

Naga was in no mood for the conversation. "And you've gotten weaker. When will you draw Fang?"

"Never, if I can help it."

"You'll die if you don't."

Kalen shook his head. "You don't know that. Our fight has been close. It is true you have the upper hand, but one slip will be your end."

Naga looked like he couldn't quite believe what he heard. He took half a step back to keep the tree between him and Sascha as she scrambled around near the top of the hill, looking for a clean shot. Kalen held out little hope. Naga was too aware of his daughter's presence and threat. She'd proven her skill with the bow in this fight, and he was proud of her, but she couldn't kill Naga.

"Is that what you think?" Naga asked.

"Anyone with eyes to watch our fight would say the same," Kalen said.

"I knew you'd gotten weaker, but I'm surprised, old friend. Your time in Bonde's lands has dulled your senses more than I expected." Naga pointed at Fang with the tip of his sword. "Draw Fang, and let us have the fight I've waited for."

Kalen raised his knife. "Make me."

He expected a wary advance, followed by a fast exchange. Instead, Naga sighed. He shouted up the hill, "Sascha, your father is being a fool. Tell him to draw Fang, or he'll die."

There was no response from the hill. Naga considered for a moment, then shrugged. "Very well, then."

He spoke runes that Kalen didn't recognize, and the sword he carried grew brighter. Then he came at Kalen with a shout.

Kalen had just enough time to realize he'd made a terrible mistake. This whole time, he thought he'd been fighting Naga at his best. But Naga had merely been testing him. The scorpion covered two paces in the time Kalen expected him to cover one, and it was all he could do to stumble back and out of the way of Naga's cut.

The tip still burned across his chest.

Naga's foot followed a blink of an eye later, stomping on Kalen's chest like he was a bug that deserved to be squashed. The kick lifted Kalen's feet off the ground and sent him flying several feet backward. An old oak was kind enough to stop his flight, and he felt his ribs crack as he slammed into the trunk. The back of his head followed a moment later, and pinpricks of light danced in his vision.

Kalen tried to keep his feet, but his legs refused to hold his weight, and he slid down the side of the trunk until he was sitting on its exposed roots. He coughed up blood.

Naga could have killed him. Kalen didn't delude himself into thinking he'd somehow avoided that cut on his own. A small adjustment would have been all that was needed to take off his head.

Naga advanced, stopping a few feet away, once again putting a tree between him and Sascha. "Now do you understand?"

Kalen couldn't find his center. He needed to protect Sascha, and he'd failed. He'd been too confident, thinking that he was enough without Fang, that the cursed sword would never need to be drawn again. But now, if he drew it as he was, it was as likely to kill him as Naga. He needed more time.

"What did you do to that sword?" he asked.

Naga held it up, letting Kalen see the runes inscribed upon the side. "You like it? I figured out how to combine Vilkas's runes with Kunama's. It hasn't seen many true tests yet, but I think it's almost as strong as Fang. Maybe even stronger. But there's only one way to find out, isn't there? What do you think?"

"Mixing runes is an abomination." It had been one of the first lessons their elders had taught them.

Naga scoffed. "An old superstition, and one that held the wolves back. Of all people, I'm surprised to hear you say such a thing. After all, how is my sword any different from your daughter?"

Kalen's eyes went wide, but he had no answer.

Wasn't that exactly what Devra had said the gods wanted her for? The mix of Bonde and Vilkas? The runes of each that lived in her? She wielded her bow with impressive skill, but Kalen thought of their passage through Devra's realm, how Sascha had sensed Devra's power in the roots.

Perhaps she lacked his strength, but her potential was so much greater than his.

He looked Naga in the eye, and he believed Naga understood. Kalen thought he'd adapted well to his life in the village, that he'd somehow matured. Now he thought that maybe he'd stayed the same, while Naga was the one who grew into a new life.

No matter. His mistakes in the past didn't change what he had to do now. For his daughter to live, Naga had to die. Fate was cruel to bring them together like this, but the gods had never been kind.

Kalen pushed himself up, using the tree that had nearly broken him as support. His legs wobbled, and his breath came in brief gasps. His ribs were broken, and who could tell what organs still worked? He searched for his center, but it was more elusive than any prey he'd ever hunted.

Why?

Naga had made himself clear. He stood as the greatest

barrier between Sascha and the rest of her life. It should have been a simple matter to find his center and draw Fang. It was the only option left to him.

He knew it.

And still, he couldn't bring himself to draw the sword.

"Please, Naga," he begged, "stand aside and let us pass. I do not want to fight you."

"If you don't draw Fang, you'll be dead before you reach the pass," Naga said. "Draw, and let our paths collide one last time."

"Please, Naga," Kalen pleaded. What could he say to change the mind of his old friend?

Naga stared at him, then shook his head. He tightened his grip on his sword until his knuckles turned white. "You're pathetic, Kalen. Even when you have everything to lose. I hope Vilkas spits on your soul for your betrayal."

"He told me to!"

Naga froze. "What did you say?"

Kalen stared at his feet, unable to meet his friend's stare. "The night before the battle, I left the camp and climbed to the highest point nearby. I prayed to Vilkas like I never had before. I was torn between my love for my brothers and sisters and my love for my wife and daughter. He appeared to me, Naga. I was his Fang, and he answered my plea."

"And he told you to leave?" Disbelief dripped from every word.

"He did! He knew that the morning battle was hopeless and that the war had been lost. I was told to flee with my wife and daughter, to make a new life among my wife's people. Vilkas said he wanted the wolves to live on, through my blood and the blood of my daughter. I was torn. Oh, my brother, you can't imagine how I was torn. But I obeyed, as I always did. Your vengeance isn't wrong, brother, but you've aimed at the wrong target. You want Vilkas to suffer, the same as I do for calling Sascha."

Naga hesitated. It was the first doubt Kalen had seen in his eyes.

Kalen dared to hope.

Then Naga shook his head, and Kalen's last hope died. "It doesn't matter. Not anymore. Have you any last words?"

"Please, Naga!"

Naga snarled, reminding Kalen of the wolf he had once been. "Pathetic!"

He raised his sword.

Then he stepped back as an arrow split the air where he'd been standing less than a heartbeat earlier. Kalen was so distracted that he'd lost track of his daughter.

Naga hadn't. A throwing knife appeared in his off hand, and he threw it up the hill. It glowed with the same soft glow his sword did.

Sascha cried out as the knife struck true.

Her cry focused Kalen the way his imminent death had failed to. He found his center, where all hesitation and doubt fell away. He could forgive Naga for almost anything, but never for this.

His hand found Fang, and he swore it cried out in relief. It was a sword meant to drink in the moonlight, to hunt for the good of the pack. Drawing Fang from its sheath, pulling it from the runes that had protected and hid it for all of Sascha's life, felt like the most natural thing in the world, like he'd been practicing daily with the blade all these years.

As soon as the blade was free, he channeled his will into the runes. He groaned as his bones knit back together and his organs returned to their proper positions. Strength flooded his limbs, and he felt like a young man again. He could run all day, fight all night, and still be ready for a sunrise adventure.

By the gods, he had missed this feeling.

He would die with Fang in his hands and thank Vilkas for the opportunity. He'd been a fool for keeping it hidden for so long.

His sharpened senses told him that Sascha was wounded but still alive, and Naga was even stronger than he'd yet revealed. Kalen rolled his shoulders back and cracked his neck. What better rebirth than to fight an opponent worthy of Fang's keen edge?

Naga held nothing back, either. He'd be a fool to do so against Fang. Kalen's sword wasn't a weapon to be tested. It was a weapon to be feared.

They strode toward one another and met in a clash of steel that echoed off the trees. Trunks shivered and creatures scattered as the two met. Both stood their ground, and the first exchange was even.

Kalen had the measure of Naga, and he was impressed. Vengeance had motivated the man in a way Vilkas's hunt never had. He'd pushed himself harder now than he had as a younger man, and the effort showed. If this had been a battle between the two men alone, Kalen wasn't sure who would stand and who would fall.

But warriors rarely fought alone. Vilkas and Kunama fought through their runes, and in this, Kunama was lacking.

In the second exchange, Kalen cut at Naga's sword instead of Naga. Runes flared to life on both swords as they clashed, so bright Kalen couldn't see the result.

But he felt it well enough.

Naga's sword shattered, releasing its stored runic strength

back into its possessor. Fang absorbed the worst of it for Kalen, but even he had to dance his feet back to keep his balance against the force.

The light faded as quickly as it had appeared. Thanks to Vilkas's runes, Kalen's sight quickly returned with the darkness.

Their positions were now reversed. Naga slumped against a tree, several of his limbs at unnatural angles. He fought for breath, and blood dribbled down his chin. The limbs were already straightening, but without his sword, it would be a full day before he could move again. Maybe more, and he'd be weak once the healing was done.

Fang cried out for blood so loudly that Kalen winced. Before he could succumb, he sheathed the sword again. His own anger and bloodlust faded, and he squatted beside his old friend. "I'm sorry it came to this."

Naga's stare was filled with venom. It took several tries for him to speak, but he forced the words out. "Kill me, you bastard."

It was the simple choice. Even without his sword, Naga was more dangerous than most scorpions.

But he was no longer any threat to Kalen.

"No. Forge a new sword if you wish, and come after me again. I owe you that much. But I will not kill you unless I have no other choice. I have shed enough blood for several lifetimes."

Kalen stood. Sascha picked her way down the steep hill. Blood on her left shoulder told Kalen where the knife had hit her. Close to the heart, but either she'd dodged or Naga had missed. He suspected Naga hadn't missed. The wound was already closing as she used Vilkas's healing runes.

"How are you?" he asked.

"Fine," she said, her voice distant.

Gods, but there was so much for them to talk about. Fortunately, they had many miles to go. They could work through her feelings of the battle together, if she let him. Otherwise, she had another long journey to walk on her own. He hoped that this once she'd let him help. "We can talk on the road, but now that I've drawn Fang, Jolon's attention will be drawn here. We need to leave, if you're well enough to travel."

She nodded but said nothing. He worried for her, but now was not the time.

"Gather as many arrows as you can. We'll leave soon."

"What about him?" Sascha asked.

"Without his sword, he's no threat to us. Especially now that I've drawn Fang. He has a family, too, and I'd rather he return to them."

Sascha drifted among the bodies, recovering what arrows hadn't been broken. They'd have to make or steal more when they got the chance. Kalen retrieved their packs from where he'd stashed them, and they were soon ready to go.

Naga watched it all without a word.

Kalen squatted down once again. Naga glared, but Kalen could live with that. He hadn't had to kill him, and that was good. "I know you hate me. And you're right to, but I sincerely hope your life is filled with blessings from this day forth. Be well, old friend."

Naga's lips curled in a snarl. "Kill me," he said.

Kalen stood and joined Sascha. He gave Naga a deep bow, then turned and left, Sascha by his side.

"KILL ME!" Naga shouted.

But Kalen kept walking and never glanced back.

FORETELLING

Sascha pulled the bowstring back to her cheek and took aim. Forty paces ahead of her, the hare looked up, its small nose sniffing the air. She called on Vilkas to steady her aim and strengthen her arm. The arrow flew true and caught the hare before it scampered away.

She stood perfectly still, bow extended and right hand near her cheek. Her attention was focused inward. There was little to notice. Her heart didn't beat faster at the successful shot, and her breathing was so even she could have been at rest. Her first hunt had made her hands sweat and her heart pound. She wanted to feel that again, but her mind and body refused.

Sascha let her arms drop. The sun would be up soon, and Dad would be waiting for her, nervously pacing around their camp.

Even thoughts of Dad, usually so reliable, failed to stir the ashes of her emotions into a flame. She'd been like this ever since the battle several days ago. They'd survived, but that night had killed something inside of her. She couldn't say what, but she felt its absence in everything she did.

The past few nights of travel had passed without incident. Channeling Vilkas's runes was easier than ever. She connected to them with barely more than a thought. She and Dad hiked steadily north, the land growing more rugged with every night. The mountains were visible now, and Dad's pace increased as they neared the northern border of Kunama lands. Every night he asked about the battle and how she felt, but she refused to answer his questions.

Sascha picked up the hare and retrieved her arrow. She wasn't opposed to discussing the battle, but she didn't know what she would say. She'd thought about little else since, but her thoughts lacked order. They felt empty.

She felt empty. Sometimes it felt like the battle had scooped everything out of her. She ran, climbed, and hunted. She made noises that barely passed for conversation. But she was nothing more than a soulless pile of flesh and bone.

Sascha returned to the camp to find Dad pacing back and forth, exactly as she'd imagined. The satisfaction of being right didn't even light a spark.

Dad already had a small fire burning. Before long, the hare was roasted, and they filled their stomachs.

Sascha hadn't been hungry, but she ate so she wouldn't have to endure more of Dad's concern. The hare was flavorless, though that was true of everything she ate or drank. Dad made appreciative noises as he bit into the meat, so she assumed the problem was with her. Most problems were with her.

They had doused the fire and were curling up to sleep

when Dad suddenly sat straight up. He looked around and sniffed the air, reminding Sascha of the hare just before she'd killed it. He came to his feet and had Fang in hand before Sascha could question him. The sword remained sheathed, but Sascha swore she could feel its power. She backed away from it.

Fang was the only thing that brought her feelings to life.

She hated that sword, more than she'd hated the sickness that had taken Mom's life too soon. It was a monster that had no place in this world, and Dad was a monster for wielding it.

She swallowed her hate. "What is it?" she asked.

"Someone's close."

Sascha didn't understand her father's preternatural senses. Even when she used Vilkas's runes to sharpen her sight and hearing, Dad noticed both predator and prey before she did. His nose picked out scents she had never smelled, and she'd never seen him surprised by his surroundings.

Just once, she wanted him to be wrong, but she suspected today wouldn't be that day. "Only one person?"

"As far as I can tell."

Without having to be asked, Sascha retreated behind him. She reached for her bow, but Dad stopped her. "I do not think she's an enemy."

As though his words had summoned her, a woman stepped from behind a rock. She had long, dark hair, but Sascha was drawn immediately to her eyes. They seemed too small and too dark to be natural. She carried a strung bow, but no arrow was set to the string. The way she walked reminded Sascha of Sonje. Both were elders accustomed to respect.

"Greetings, wanderers," the woman said. Her voice was stronger than Sascha expected, carrying easily to their ears.

"And to you," Dad answered.

The woman stepped into their campsite and sat down as if she had camped there through the entire night with them. She gestured for them to sit. Dad looked around and sniffed the air, then obeyed. Sascha followed Dad's lead.

"My name is Gossa. I'm an elder in service of Azeria," the woman said. She fixed Dad with a pointed stare. "And you must be Kalen, Fang of Vilkas."

Dad was wary but nodded. "Does Azeria contest this land?"

"No, though, you'll soon enter our territory. We control most of what once belonged to Vilkas."

"I would pass in peace, if you permit," Dad said.

"It is why I have come. Vilkas has called the girl, hasn't he?"

"Sascha, and yes, he has."

"I would cast for her."

Just when Sascha was about to lose her temper about them speaking about her like she wasn't there, Dad gestured to her. "Her blood, her choice."

Gossa faced her and offered a quick bow of her head. "Azeria seeks guidance regarding this conflict, and they have sent me to cast the runes over you."

After her last few experiences with the runes, Sascha wasn't sure Gossa should. "The last time runes were cast, they started a fire in the caster's tent."

Gossa's gaze shot to Dad, who nodded. "He was young and wasn't aware of the strength of her blood. He cast wooden runes."

Gossa sniffed as though insulted. "You need not fear,

Sascha. I have cast for some of the greatest warriors in the world for three times the years you've been alive. My cast will reveal only truth."

"What consequences do I risk with my decision?" she asked.

Far from being insulted by the question, Gossa smiled widely. "An unusually wise question for one so young." The elder looked to Dad. "You've raised her well."

Dad chuckled grimly. "Any wisdom she possesses, she came by on her own. Nothing I did had anything to do with it."

At least he understood that much.

Gossa took a deep breath. "If you refuse, the future is murky. My clan's runemasters have sensed the fight between wolf and scorpion and are uneasy. There is no love lost between Azeria and Kunama, but the scorpions are numerous, and their runemasters are strong. I do not know if we would aid the wolf or the scorpion."

"Is that a threat?" Sascha growled.

"You may perceive it as one, but I'm not committing to any particular path. The other elders and I have a choice to make, and we hope the casting will aid us in this choice. If we do not cast, I cannot say which direction we will travel."

"And the risks of casting?" Sascha asked.

"Azeria's alliance will still be in question, but I would inform you of my counsel before I leave you. My word carries much weight among the elders. Otherwise, it is the same risk that all castings carry. You will have to bear the burden of the truth."

Sascha looked to Dad, expecting guidance, but he offered none.

After her previous experiences, the wise choice seemed

to be a refusal, but her curiosity wouldn't be denied. "Cast for me then, please."

Gossa reached into her cloak and pulled out a pouch. From it, she removed a white square of linen embroidered with runes along its edges. It reminded Sascha of the cloth Sonje used, though the runes were different and far more numerous. The cloth itself was larger, too. Dried bloodstains showed a lifetime's worth of casting.

A sudden doubt seized Sascha. "What if the scorpions find out where we are?" she asked Dad.

"They already know. Now that Fang has been drawn, Jolon will find me. But a valid concern, nevertheless."

Gossa dumped her runes into her hands. They were small and white. Sascha squinted and realized they were bones. Gossa noticed her stare and held one up for examination. "Bones from my master."

Sascha felt the blood drain from her face, but Gossa laughed. "Not something you'll ever see in the land of Bonde, I wager, but common enough in these parts. Stronger than stone, if the soul that resided in these bones was strong enough in life."

The elder took out a small needle. "Will you, or shall I?"

Sascha took the needle and pricked her smallest finger. Gossa collected the blood, using far less than Angar had. When she had enough, she shook the bones in her hands, coating them all.

Gossa spoke softly, and Sascha felt the surrounding air grow even colder. The change didn't bother Gossa, and she cast the runes.

Sascha flinched away, though nothing happened. The runes came to rest on the cloth, and Gossa leaned forward. To the side, Dad did the same.

Gossa studied the pattern for a long while. Sascha couldn't understand Azeria's runes, so she settled for drawing her clues from the elder's expression. Unfortunately, the woman was almost as unreadable as her creepy bones.

Finally, Gossa picked up the four corners of the cloth and returned the cloth and runes to the bag. She sat back and fixed Sascha with a contemplative stare.

"What did they say?" Sascha asked.

"I never said I would tell you what they said. I said only I would tell you what I would counsel the other elders."

Sascha stood. It was hard to care about any of this. She was tired, so tired. She missed her bed and wanted to sleep in it until the harvest was over. "Fine," she said.

"You're in a dangerous place," Gossa said.

"Trust me, I know. The scorpions want to kill me, the weather wants to kill me, and now your clan probably does, too. If this goes on much longer, maybe I'll just do everyone a favor and jump off one of those cliffs."

She imagined it, and it was so real she could feel the wind blowing through her hair. A few precious moments of freedom followed by a final, blissful silence.

"It's not others that I speak of, Sascha, but yourself. Your spirit hovers on the border between life and death, teetering from one to the other. Why?"

"Didn't the runes tell you?"

"They did, but it means nothing if the words don't come from your lips."

Sascha swallowed the lump in her throat. She was torn between going to sleep and answering Gossa's question. Again, she looked at Gossa and thought of Sonje. She'd turned countless times to the older woman for advice, and she'd never led Sascha astray.

"I see little point in living if it's all about killing."

The elder was on her feet and next to Sascha before Sascha realized what was happening. Gossa embraced her, and though the woman was a stranger, Sascha collapsed into her arms. She felt like she had when Mom had died, when there didn't seem to be anything worth waking up for.

The moment of weakness passed, and Sascha gently disentangled herself.

Gossa gestured for her to sit again, and Sascha relented. "Let me tell you some of what I see," she said.

Sascha wiped the tears from her eyes and nodded for Gossa to continue.

"There is much you probably already know. Though your destination draws near, the path before you is harder than the journey behind you. Your initiation will test you harder than you can imagine. It will be all the harder because you aren't a trueborn daughter of Vilkas. Your success is anything but certain. But if you pass the rite, you'll become a force of nature.

"Before you even reach the tree, though, you must overcome another challenge. You need to decide if your life is worth living. If it's worth fighting for. You follow this path because your father set you upon it. As your father, he wants nothing more than for you to live and thrive. So it is for any father who cares for his daughter. But the battle you fought is nothing but a small taste of the choices you'll face if you pass Vilkas's trials. Only you can decide if you want to live such a life. If not, better you follow through on your empty threat and jump off a cliff. Enjoy the last moments of your freedom."

Dad objected, but Gossa cut him off with a glare.

"There is incredible potential within you, but such potential requires a matching effort. There is no shame in admitting you aren't strong enough to shoulder such a burden."

Gossa stroked her chin. "One more insight I would share. Many live their lives believing they will someday be easier. The runes see no such future for you. Once, long ago, Kalen chose the path of ease and comfort, and he will suffer for that choice until his dying day. If you choose life, it'll never be easy."

"Is this supposed to be encouraging?" Sascha asked.

"It's supposed to be true. What you make of it is entirely up to you."

Gossa stood. "Thank you for allowing me to cast for you. It has been... revealing."

"What will you tell your elders?" Sascha asked.

"To let you pass in peace. I do not know what you will choose, but what I've seen from you today and in your runes convinces me I would rather entrust our futures to you than to Kunama."

After everything else, the support surprised Sascha. She bowed her head in thanks, her thoughts swirling.

Gossa and Dad bowed to one another, and then the elder left without so much as another word. She and Dad were alone again, and it was as if they'd never had a visitor. Only the blood on her small finger served as proof that any of it had happened.

Dad watched her but said nothing. After a while, she couldn't stand the silence. "What do you think?" she asked.

"Hard words for a father to hear," Dad said. He scratched

his neck. "I believe she believes she is telling the truth, but I never put too much trust in the runes."

"Why not?"

"I put little trust in the gods that control them. Everyone I knew and loved when I was small died thanks to Vilkas. Hard to trust after that."

"What do you think I should do?"

Dad grimaced as if he'd been stung. "I'm starting to think it's not up to me to decide what you should do. I want the same things I've always wanted for you, and that's for you to leave all of this behind and be free. Only now, I'm realizing that being free means letting you go, too. You can't fly if I'm holding on too tight."

She bobbed her head, and the thoughts that had plagued her finally faded. She had no answers, not yet. But she felt at ease for now, and that was enough.

She yawned and stretched. "Thanks," she said.

"Any time."

She curled up and fell asleep, dreaming of flight.

FAILURE

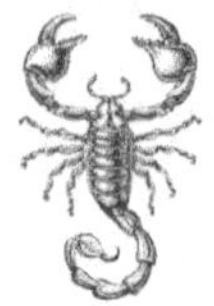

Naga's bones and flesh knit together slowly, leaving him plenty of time to consider his failure. Master would be furious. Of that, there was no doubt. The only way to snuff out Master's displeasure would be to chase after Kalen and kill him. Naga knew his old friend's destination, and his daughter slowed him. Even with their lead, he could catch them before they reached the border.

Catching them was pointless, though.

He laughed bitterly. Life was never fair. He'd spent nearly every day since the destruction of the wolves honing his skills. He'd combined the best of Kunama's runes with the most dangerous of Vilkas's. Combat and trials were the only constants in his life. He'd pulled and clawed his way through the ranks until he enjoyed Master's favor.

Kalen had rested, most likely in Bonde's lands, growing weak as he feasted on the labors of others.

Naga should have won. And he would have, if not for Fang. That cursed blade was too strong for this world, strengthened by all the blood it had consumed over the years.

There was nothing he could do alone.

Once he could walk, he returned to Master's winter camp. He planned to fall to his knees and plead for another chance. Master rarely gave them, but Naga was one of his strongest warriors, who'd proven his loyalty twice as often as those born scorpions. With another sword and another hunting party, Naga might yet prove victorious.

He hadn't made it halfway back to camp when he felt Master's presence. Master's strength carried on the air, apparent to all who were sensitive to runes.

Kalen's drawing of Fang had pulled Master from the protection of his camp. Naga's shame doubled, that his failure had brought Master to this. Winter camp was a time of rest, yet Master marched north.

He reached Master's hunting party near nightfall. They'd set up camp already. A dozen of Kunama's finest warriors circled the tents, and the power of the assembled runemasters was palpable. Naga's hairs stood on end as he approached.

The warriors recognized him on sight and let him pass. A bitter wind blew from the north, and Naga was grateful for the shelter of the tents. He made his way straight for the largest tent in the center of the circle. At the entrance, he took a knee before the two guards and waited for permission to enter.

If Master granted him these forces, Naga would bring back Kalen's head within days. Strong as Fang was, Kalen was still just one man, and his daughter was weak. Every warrior here carried a weapon etched with runes, and all possessed at least some skill with Kunama's power. Kalen was doomed. He just hadn't realized it yet.

A runemaster emerged from the tent and bade Naga to enter. Naga did so, crawling on hands and knees as was appropriate. Nearly the entire summer had passed since he'd seen Master in person. Once inside the tent, he pressed his forehead to the ground, then sat back on his knees.

He always forgot, when he was gone for a time, how small of a man Master was in person. His legend loomed large across the land, but the top of his head barely reached Naga's chest when Naga was standing. Naga wondered how many opponents had felt a false confidence as they faced Master.

Naga had, a long time ago. To this day, he'd never been so easily beaten. Any who underestimated Master paid for their folly before long.

Little about Master had changed over the past season. He still radiated a sense of strength and command. His short black hair was dark as night, and his gray eyes looked as though he was gazing at two worlds at once. He wore simple traveling clothes. Nothing on his person gave any hint that he was the most powerful person in the world.

When he spoke, his voice was soft but laced with menace. "Naga. You failed me."

Naga bowed his head. "He proved stronger in our first battle. Give me but one more chance, and I will bring his head to you. There is no need to trouble yourself over one so insignificant as him."

"I will decide what is significant and what is not. He drew Fang against you, didn't he?"

"I was about to kill him, and he had no choice."

"Every runemaster within days of the duel felt him draw

the sword. Its power rivals even my own. What makes you think that if I granted you another chance, your second attempt would prove any more successful than your first?"

"I know where he is going, and there may still be a chance to ambush him before he reaches his destination. His loyalty to what I once was makes him weak against me. He should have killed me when he had me at his mercy, but he could not strike the killing blow."

"Where is he going?"

"To Vilkas's tree. His daughter has been called, which is why he's fled his hiding place."

Master's eyes narrowed at the new information. "How certain are you of this? What if it is only a deception to draw me forward?"

Paranoia glittered beneath the surface of Master's eyes, and it frightened Naga. Master was as strong as the gods, but he feared Kalen, and Kalen alone. It made him prone to impulsive choices.

Naga bowed his head to hide his innermost thoughts from Master. "I do not think Kalen would lie to me, Master. I believe him."

Master paced before him. "What would you ask of me?"

"One last chance, Master. I'll need a rune sword and at least half a dozen warriors. Give me that, and I'll return Kalen's head to you."

Master stopped his pacing. "Your emotions betray you, Naga. You return, knowing I cannot tolerate failure. You ask for more, even as you know, deep in your heart, that it won't be enough to defeat Kalen. Your old friend is your better, but you refuse to acknowledge this simple truth. So why do you waste my time?"

Naga's insides turned to ice. He'd known returning was a

risky plan, but it was the only one with a chance of success. If he wasn't careful, this meeting would also end his life. What could he say that wouldn't offend Master?

He pushed down his fear and kept his voice steady. "I would rather die in your service than live with failure. Kalen has shamed me."

"Indeed, he has. And your shame reflects on me."

Naga never saw Master's move. One moment he stood before Naga, then Naga blinked, and he was gone. Something pricked him in the back of the neck, and then Master stood before him again. Naga tried to raise his hand to the back of his neck, but it refused to listen to his commands.

Kunama's sting.

He'd heard of the technique but never seen it firsthand. He wouldn't move again unless Master saw fit to heal him. Fear clutched at his heart. This wasn't how he'd imagined the meeting would go.

Master kneeled in front of Naga so they could face each other. "If you wanted to die in my service, the answer was simple. Chase after Kalen and find some way to kill him. Instead, you come running back to me, hoping that I'll grant you the strength you lack."

Master shook his head. "You disappoint me, Naga. When I adopted you, I saw a glorious future ahead. You were the strength Kunama needed at the time we most needed it. But failure has no place in the world we're building. You retreated, and if there is one rule scorpions hold sacred, it is that we never go back. We must always move forward, no matter the challenge."

Master stood and sighed. "Normally, a failure such as yours would be met with public humiliation. But I will honor the service you've given me for all these years. Your death will be a private one, right here in my tent. I've even brought you companions for your last journey."

Master motioned, and some of his servants entered the tent. Each carried a head in their hands. One by one, they laid the heads of his children in front of him, starting with his eldest son and ending with his beautiful, precious daughter. His wife was last. The servants bowed, then departed.

"Be thankful," Master said, "for I ordered swift deaths for them all. In the morning, when your lungs and heart have finally given out, you may join them so that my warriors may see my mercy as well as my discipline."

Master threw on a heavy cloak. Outside, the wind howled down the mountains, as though furious at the crimes committed within Master's camp. Master offered the briefest bow of his head. "Rest well, Naga. It was an honor having your service for the years I did."

Then Naga was alone with what remained of his family. The greatest gift he'd ever received. Greater by far than any sword Master had granted him.

That night, he discovered that Kunama's sting didn't stop tears from falling.

BORDER

Sascha had heard tales of mountains aplenty, but standing among them made her feel like an ant in the land of giants. Bonde's lands were filled with gently rolling hills and flat plains. More often than not, she could see to distant horizons and watch animals and people that were hundreds and thousands of paces away. The vastness of the plains made her feel small, too, but not like this. Plains made her realize how much land there was. Mountains reminded her that the world she walked was more powerful than she imagined. Its strength thrust these enormous monuments upward to the sky.

Hiking was harder here, and the mere act of breathing was an effort. Their paths remained clear, but snow built near the summit of the mountains. The highest mountains were jagged peaks, stabbing like knives into the sky.

It was a beautiful land, but one Sascha decided wasn't for her. This was a place where one had to fight the land itself to survive. Where food was nearly impossible to come by. The slight hunting skills she'd developed on their journey failed her, and Dad hunted most of their food.

Today her feet and legs ached, and as the night fell, they'd called an early stop. After their meeting with Gossa, they'd walked for a full night and day, altering the nocturnal pattern that had carried them safely through Kunama's lands. Dad claimed they weren't likely to encounter many scorpions this far north and that the daylight would make traveling in the mountains easier.

Sascha didn't think Dad told the full truth, but she didn't push. She much preferred walking in the daylight here, and she slept better at night.

She'd already set up their camp and prepared a small fire. Now all that remained was for Dad to return with some food to eat. Their supplies were running low. If they could have risked stopping for a few days, they could have killed something larger and dried the meat, but their pace was relentless. Some days, when Sascha fell asleep, she dreamed of going to bed and sleeping for whole moons.

While she waited, she focused on a small patch of grass fighting for survival in the meager soil. As she ran her hand across it, she could sense some of the same strength that had been clear to her in Dreva's passages. The world was alive, and she was just waking up to that knowledge.

The grass here was weak and close to death. She placed her hand on the grass and whispered. As she connected a sliver of her will to the rune, the grass turned greener and grew taller. She smiled at her success. She had little time away from Dad, but what little she had, she used to practice the skills he hadn't taught her. The same repetition that had served her so well with Vilkas's runes worked here as well.

Sascha sensed Dad before she heard or saw him, a feat

that was becoming more common as she grew in power. Against the life that bloomed around her, he was a darkness on the prowl. His aura frightened her more than she cared to admit. He'd never struck her, and she wanted to believe he never would, but that darkness told another story. At his heart, Dad was a man of violence.

She turned her attention from the grass, but not in time. He'd been close enough to notice, and she cursed her own distraction.

He joined her by the fire. He'd killed two hares, and together they prepared the meal.

"What were you doing?" he asked.

She knew no lie would fool him. Chances were, he'd already guessed at least most of it. She understood a little better now why he hadn't lied to Naga back in the clearing. It achieved nothing and showed only disrespect. "Practicing Dreva's runes."

"That was what she spoke with you about before we parted?"

"It was."

"Can you tell me what you learned?"

Sascha debated. Dreva had said nothing about keeping the rune a secret, but she'd seen well enough how tightly other runemasters held onto their knowledge. By that measure, it felt like something to be kept close.

But Dad had also shared as much of his learning as she'd been able to absorb, and the nature of Dreva's rune wasn't one that demanded secrecy. If anything, more people in the world needed to know it. "It's a rune of both healing and growth."

Dad didn't disguise his interest. "How powerful is it? Can it bring the dead back to life?"

Sascha shook her head. "I don't think so. Once past the veil of this world, nothing returns. I've only used it on plants so far, but I'm confident it would work on people as well. It's not too different from Vilkas's healing runes."

Dad got the meat roasting over the fire. Sascha read his aura, which she was learning revealed more of a person's emotions than their face. The darkness that surrounded him revealed little, though. "You're not upset, are you?"

Dad looked up, and surprise flashed through his aura. "Not at all. If anything, I'm a little jealous."

She hadn't expected that. "Why? Would you like me to show you it?"

"I would be honored, but it will do me little good."

"Why?"

"Vilkas's runes are the only ones I can use. I'm not sure why, but I suspect it has something to do with the fact that I served as his Fang for so long. Other runemasters can use runes of other gods, but it's a skill that has always eluded me. When you touched the roots of the world in Dreva's passage, you felt something, didn't you?"

"It was like being a part of the entire world at once. It was incredible."

"I touched the same roots and didn't feel a thing."

She studied Dad and tried to understand the subtle changes in his aura. She saw disappointment, but not in the ways she would have guessed. "You gave everything to Vilkas, didn't you?"

Dad poked at the coals with a stick. "At the time, it was the quickest route to the strength my clan needed. I was like you, always eager to learn everything, but I was forced to focus on what was most essential. Vilkas rewarded loyalty, so that was the path I took. My devotion gave me a strength no one else could match, but it cut off branches of knowledge I would have loved to explore. It was annoying then, but frustrating now."

She wondered why he claimed to have no regrets about his choices when his aura told another story entirely. He'd given everything to the wolves, only to see them collapse. Then he pretended to be a peaceful farmer, only to have it snatched away from him. She didn't have the courage to ask him, though.

He interrupted her thoughts. "Would you be willing to show me Dreva's rune and show me how you use it?"

"Of course." The meat of the hare was just beginning to darken, so it would be a bit before it was ready to eat.

She looked around for something to demonstrate on. Her eye settled on a desiccated, thorny bush. She walked over to it and waited for Dad to stand beside her. She began once he had a clear view.

Sascha gently put her hand on one of the bush's limbs and closed her eyes. It was thin and dry, so weak she could snap it between her fingers with ease. Instead of doing that, she let some of her will trickle into the plant and listened to its story. It had thrived in the rainy season and stored up moisture for the dry season, but the length of the drought had sapped it of most of its water. It teetered on the brink of death.

She imagined water returning, filling the bush like a cup. When she had the idea firmly fixed in her mind, she connected her will to Dreva's rune. Her will became water and restored the bush to full health. When she opened her eyes, the bush was green and flowering. She squeezed and twisted the limb she'd been holding, avoiding the thorns. It bent but didn't snap.

Sascha exhaled gently and grinned. She appreciated what Vilkas's runes allowed her to accomplish, but mastering Dreva's rune gave her a deeper sense of satisfaction.

Dad's reaction surprised her. He dropped to a knee and ran his hands along the healed bush, careful not to let his hands get cut. His eyes were wide, and the corner of his mouth was turned up.

When he looked at her, he smiled widely. "Incredible."

She understood he wasn't only referring to the healing. She blushed and wasn't sure what to say.

Dad stood and placed his enormous hand on her shoulder. "I'm proud of you."

For a moment, it felt like all was right with the world.

The next day's climbing was difficult. A wide path weaved back and forth up the side of a mountain, but Dad ignored that path in favor of a narrow one that made a straighter line to the peaks. They ascended through mountain meadows and up perilous routes. At times, they scrambled on all fours, half climbing and half walking. Dad took to it naturally, revealing more of his upbringing.

Sascha didn't find it so easy. It took a constant amount of focus to remain connected to Vilkas's runes and an additional amount to carefully place her hands and feet. The path exposed them to sheer drops. Her palms grew sweaty, and she imagined herself falling to her doom. More than once, she cursed Dad for dragging her out here, though she knew it was unfair of her.

As Dad leaped from one stone to another, Sascha

wondered what it had been like for him growing up here. The terrain seemed unsafe for a child, but clearly it had served the wolves well enough.

The exposed sections of the trail never lasted long, thankfully. Before long, the trail would grow wider or level out, and Sascha's attitude would switch directions like smoke drifting in the wind. The views from the trail stunned her.

The highest she'd been in her life prior to this trip was the treetops in the grove outside their village. Two or three were ideal for climbing, and she'd thrilled at the feeling of being three and four times as tall as Dad.

Those achievements seemed pitiful now. Incredible vistas stretched out before her, her sight stretching farther than it ever had. Dark green pine trees topped the peaks of the foothills below, and beyond that lay the rolling hills and plains they'd spent so long traversing.

At one stop, she asked if they could see Bonde's lands. Dad shook his head, and she marveled at the fact they had traveled as far as they had. She understood they had traveled vast distances every day, but it wasn't until the land stretched out before her she understood just how far they had come.

That afternoon, Dad slowed for no apparent reason. Their treacherous path had joined again with the wider horse trail as it continued its climb into the mountains. Sascha looked left and right, expecting trouble, but she sensed nothing out of the ordinary. Dad's senses remained sharper, but she closed the gap between them daily.

Dad came to a complete stop. She halted beside him, but her question died on her lips as she looked at his face. He was pale as a sheet.

She looked around again but saw nothing that frightened her.

"What's wrong?" she asked.

He pointed toward a pile of stone sitting near the edge of the path. Sascha followed his finger but still didn't understand. "What?"

He swallowed hard. "This used to be the border for Vilkas's lands. We should have been safe here."

He wasn't making sense. Sascha approached the stones and squatted down beside them. Up close, she saw many of the stones were unnaturally smooth on one side. That same side had patterns carved in it. She guessed that at one point, the stones had been a pillar, and she understood. This had once been Vilkas's boundary marker.

Dad had come home only to find it destroyed.

She ran the tips of her fingers over the stone. Once, the pillar might have been filled with power, but those times were long past. The boundary marker was nothing but stone now.

She tried to imagine how Dad would feel. She thought of returning to the village, only to find all the homes destroyed and the people gone.

Dad had known, of course. He'd fled the last battle of his people, knowing they were sentenced to death. Even so, it was one thing to know and another to experience. It wouldn't matter if she'd been warned about her village's destruction. Seeing the devastation in person would still wound her.

She walked slowly ahead to give Dad time and space. Heavy as the burden was, he would want to carry it on his own, the same as always. She waited up ahead for him.

When he finally arrived, there was no trace of the distress he'd shown before. "Sorry about that," he said.

She started to tell him there was nothing to apologize for,

but he continued before she could speak. "It shouldn't have been a surprise to me, but I always assumed the land would remain unchanged, even if the wolves no longer hunted it. I don't know whose land this is now. We'll have to be careful."

Sascha wondered if perhaps this entire journey had been a fool's errand. How could Vilkas call her when he couldn't even control this stretch of land?

She didn't bother asking. That was a worry she didn't need to burden Dad with. So she nodded, and together she and Dad sought what remained of Vilkas's land.

ALLIANCE

Kalen's return to his homeland unleashed an unexpected flood of emotions. He tried to mask and ignore them, but he might as well have drained a flooded field with a leaky cup. Sascha's eyes kept drifting over him, and he suspected she was gaining the ability to sense his aura.

If raising her before hadn't been tough enough, it was going to become downright impossible soon.

He shoved that thought away hard. His well-intentioned desire to raise Sascha well caused many of their troubles. She didn't need him guiding her every step she took. She was competent enough to find her own way.

Most of the time.

Right now, she was doing better than him. He thought he was prepared for the sight of his homeland, but he wasn't. He believed he had put the past behind him, but it was more like he had shoved it into a small closet. Now he was opening the closet door and letting it all crash around him.

They passed a tree he and his friends had climbed when

they were young and the hunt had taken them close to the southern border. They'd climbed and looked south, telling each other stories of how they would become fierce hunters and expand Vilkas's land southward.

Of those friends, only he remained. Most had died before the last battle, but two others had lived to march to their deaths that day without him.

The sight of the tree flushed his cheeks with shame, even though it was just a damned tree. He hurried past it, grateful Sascha didn't bother him with questions.

The same scene repeated itself throughout the day. He knew this land better than he knew his daughter. He'd explored it every day of his youth, roaming far and wide with his pack. Every turn in the path revealed another memory, and every memory served as another reminder that he had lived while his pack had died.

The wind howled down the pass as they ascended, carrying the screams of ghosts. The wolves had died out, but no other clan took its place. He saw no tracks, no sign of humanity.

Why had the other clans fought so hard if they weren't even going to claim the spoils of their victory? Why had his pack been slaughtered?

He was so distracted by thoughts of the past that Sascha noticed the watchers before he did. Her gaze traveled to a ridgeline above them. Kalen followed her gaze and saw a handful of warriors keeping pace with them high above. They carried bows, but their arrows remained in their quivers.

Kalen cursed and searched for cover, but there was none to be found. "Stay close," he said.

Sascha obeyed, and Kalen came to a stop. He counted six

archers, all of whom stopped when he did. He studied the terrain. The archers weren't as safe as they imagined. If he drew Fang, he could be among them quickly. Not fast enough to prevent them from at least one volley, but if he was moving, they would target him instead of Sascha. So long as he survived the first wave of arrows, he could kill them before they launched a second.

Sascha put a hand on his arm. "Don't," she said. He looked back, annoyed that she continued to read his intentions with such ease.

"I don't think they mean us any harm," she explained.

"That's not a chance we can take," Kalen said.

"It is," Sascha argued.

Before they could resolve their differences, another visitor appeared on the trail thirty paces ahead of them. Kalen swallowed his mounting shame. His distraction had caused him to miss her as well. But her figure was familiar, and Kalen's thoughts howled at the betrayal.

Sascha tightened her grip on his arm. "Peace, Dad."

She stepped forward and away from his protection.

Kalen looked up, expecting the archers to take the opportunity. But they remained still and watchful. Sascha spoke loudly enough for her voice to carry, both to the woman blocking their way and to the archers above. "Gossa, it is good to see you again, but why are you here?"

The old woman gave the slightest of bows. "For a cup of tea, if you'd join us."

Kalen growled. His hand stretched toward Fang, ready to take his chances with the archers.

Sascha's response kept him still. "We are in a great rush, as you know. As wonderful as tea sounds, there is no time."

"There's even less than you think, which is why we've

come. Jolon rides here, driving horses to exhaustion and beyond. He'll reach the tree in days."

Kalen swore out loud. They'd come too far to be turned away. "Then let us through! Every moment we talk is a moment Sascha isn't in that tree!"

Sascha's head snapped around. "What did you say?"

"Come, Kalen. We know a shortcut that will grant you another day," Gossa said.

It felt like a trap. "I spent every day of my childhood in these lands. There are no shortcuts."

"You roamed wild under the light of the moon and the watchful eye of the sun. You know nothing of burrowing or the caves that run beneath your feet. We can have you to the tree by tomorrow, if you join us. I can't promise you the full three days, but it's as much as we can do."

"Three days?" Sascha's head snapped back to Gossa, her voice getting higher. "What are you talking about?"

Gossa frowned. "He hasn't told you?"

"He never tells me anything!"

Kalen grimaced but relaxed and let his hand fall away from Fang. Gossa had him in a corner. He suspected the archers weren't a random assortment of young warriors but some of her best. Their only option was to follow. "Then lead the way."

Sascha turned and glared, but Kalen pretended to ignore her. The cost of his silence was about to come due again, and he didn't look forward to paying it.

Gossa made a gesture, and the archers came down from the ridge. "The path we take is narrow at first, but you should fit. Follow us."

They followed the trail for a while longer, then one archer split off and climbed higher. The others followed, with Kalen bringing up the end of the line. He kept his senses sharp. He was inclined to trust Gossa, but after having to fight Naga, his trust was fragile.

They picked their way up the craggy slope until the lead archer squeezed through a crack in the stone. The others followed, disappearing into the mountain as though the crack was a ravenous mouth. Sascha followed the foxes before Kalen could object, leaving only him and Gossa alone on the mountain.

Gossa stopped him. "For a man who has fought in so many battles, your fear surprises me."

"Is it fear to want something different for her?"

"Of course not, but fear is the reason you have kept as much from her as you have."

Kalen clenched his fist and growled, but one of Embla's sayings rose in his memory and kept him from lashing out.

We get most angry at the words we secretly fear are true.

When no other response was forthcoming, Gossa shrugged. "I'll follow behind to cast runes of protection. The way will be narrow for you, but I believe you'll fit."

Kalen stared into the crack the others had disappeared within. All he saw was darkness. To his eyes, it didn't look like it was more than a few feet deep. He turned sideways and shuffled in.

His breaths immediately grew shallow as the rock enclosed him. He tried to breathe deep and calm himself, but the stone pressed against both his chest and back. The crack only allowed shallow breaths. He forced himself deeper into the crack, and the stone squeezed tighter.

Then he could go no further. His chest and ribs could barely expand with his rapid breathing, and no matter how he shuffled and angled his feet, his body wouldn't move. He tried to retreat but to no avail.

"I'm stuck!" he croaked.

He was going to die, trapped between two stones like a damned fool.

"Suck everything in," Gossa commanded.

He tried, and his feet pressed against the stone floor. He reached out with his arm, seeking any form of handhold that he could pull on.

Gossa whispered and pushed with surprising strength. His body shifted, and someone grabbed his free hand and pulled.

With Gossa pushing and an archer pulling, Kalen finally squeezed through the crack and emerged into a wider space. He took a deep breath and put his hands on his knees. Slowly, his heart stopped pounding in his chest. Complete, thought-freezing terror gave way to mild panic.

He looked around and saw a faint flicker of firelight. Here the crack widened and bent, forming a tunnel he could crawl through. He followed the archer who had pulled him.

They emerged into a small chamber barely large enough for Kalen to stand. The other archers and Sascha were gathered there. Two of the foxes carried small torches and, once all were assembled, led the way deeper into the mountain.

Their journey proved the truth of Gossa's words above. Kalen would have sworn that he knew this land as well as anyone alive, but that was true only of the surface. Wolves prowled the night, but they weren't meant for the dark passages underground hidden from the sight of the moon.

The tunnel branched and rejoined several times, creating a maze Kalen was certain he would never find his way through. The underground lacked all that he relied on to find his way in the world. There were no stars, no moon, and no wind to guide the way. He didn't doubt the foxes knew exactly where they went, though. The archers in the lead took every turn without hesitation, and Kalen soon felt the power of Vilkas's tree ahead.

One last section challenged Kalen. It forced him onto his belly, pulling himself through another small crack that led to another tunnel that connected to a cave he knew well. He'd played in the cave countless times as a child and spent several nights sleeping within.

He went to the mouth of the cave and looked out, amazed at the familiar sight. He thought he knew the cave well, but he'd never guessed a web of passages could be found through the crack in the dark tunnels. Gossa had been right, though. The passage had shaved a day off their journey. The tree wasn't far ahead. They could be there tomorrow with little difficulty.

The thought gave him pause. All this time traveling should have given him time to prepare himself for the sacrifice to come, but it hadn't. Somewhere in the back of his mind, he'd hoped that another path would present itself. He'd held out an impossible hope.

"We need to talk, Dad," Sascha said as she came to stand beside him.

"Suppose we do," Kalen admitted. "Where would you like me to start?"

"What exactly is the initiation?"

"It's the rite of passage all wolves must go through to become runemasters." There was more, of course, but he couldn't bring himself to answer her completely.

"Why must I go through it?"

He grimaced. "Most wolves had a choice. Anyone can become a runemaster, if their will is strong enough. Some born of strong runemasters didn't have the choice. The power gets into blood and bone, and if parents are strong enough, they pass that power down to their children. Those children must become runemasters, or the power devours them from within. That is happening to you."

"You've been training me this whole journey. Isn't that enough?"

"I wish it was. There is knowledge here," Kalen tapped his head, "and there is *knowing* here." He tapped his chest.

"You've learned plenty, but not enough to control the power growing within you. There's nothing I can teach you that would help. We must learn some lessons a different way, and that's what the initiation does."

"What happens during the initiation? What do I need to do?"

Finally, there was nothing left to hide behind. "All you need to do is survive."

"What?" The anger in her voice was barely controlled.

"Tomorrow, we will reach the tree that is the heart of Vilkas's power in this world. It will open up, much the way Dreva's tree did back in the sanctuary. You will step inside." Kalen paused and took a deep breath. "I can't tell you what will happen within, not because it's a secret, but because the experience is different for everyone. The initiation is a series of trials, of suffering beyond your imagining. Passing each trial requires a deeper understanding of the power of runes. If you survive, you'll be much stronger than before."

At first, Kalen thought Sascha had taken the explanation well. She was still and quiet. Then she turned on him, and the fierceness of her stare made him retreat a pace. Tears formed at the corners of her eyes.

"How long?" she growled.

"Time passes differently within. It is always three days out here, but within, it feels like longer."

Her voice was soft but venomous. "You brought me all this way just to throw me in a tree so I could suffer *for three days*!"

Half a dozen defenses flashed through his thoughts, but before he could choose the best, she was gone. She ran out of the cave and away from him. He started after her, but a thin hand grabbed his wrist. He looked back to see Gossa.

"Let her run, Kalen. I will follow. Sometimes, the words a child most needs to hear can't come from a parent."

Kalen felt like all the air had been punched from his lungs. He sagged, then nodded. It felt like his responsibility, but he was glad to share the burden with another.

He slunk back toward the fire the foxes had started. They shared their meat with him, but it was tasteless. He ate until he could eat no more, then found a corner of the cave he'd used to sleep in when he was younger.

The world had seemed so much more full of possibility then.

EDGE OF LIFE AND DEATH

Sascha left the cave. A well-worn path snaked down the side of the mountain, but she spotted a fainter one that climbed even higher. She took that path, wanting the solace and perspective of altitude. Eventually, the path ended at a boulder that overlooked the peaks and valleys. She plopped down on the stone and wiped the tears from her cheeks.

For a long time, she did nothing but stare into the distance. Dad would chase her down before long, and there would be another fight. But for now, she didn't want to think, didn't want to reason her way through life. She wanted only space and quiet.

Qualities her overlook excelled at.

In time, the storm of emotions subsided. The mountains cast a spell of their own, calming her like nothing else could. Before their size, grandeur, and age, her own problems were insignificant.

She heard footsteps on the path below, but they weren't Dad's. Gossa appeared soon after. "Mind if I join you?" she asked.

The peace had been nice while it lasted.

Sascha gestured to the boulder and scooted over so there was space for the older woman. Gossa nodded gratefully and took the offered seat.

Sascha expected some sort of lecture or a question, but Gossa just sat. They enjoyed the view together until Sascha broke the silence. "Have you lived here long?"

"It doesn't always feel that way, but when you get to be as old as I am, time plays tricks on you. Days seem to pass in the blink of an eye, and years disappear every time you turn your head. But my family has called these lands home for the better part of ten years."

Sascha balanced the numbers in her head, comparing them to the parts of Dad's history she now understood. "That's shorter than since the wolves were destroyed."

"True. The clans came together to kill Vilkas, but it was about the only time we ever agreed on anything. As soon as we won the battle, we turned on each other. There were years of battle. Brought no small number of us to our knees, but we fought on. Eventually, we won the rights to this territory."

"Were you the ones who destroyed the border stone?"

"No. Scorpions did that. Same as they do everywhere they conquer. Kunama wants everything for himself. Doesn't want to leave any trace of the other gods."

"Why?"

Gossa snorted. "You go into that tree tomorrow, you can ask Vilkas yourself, though I'm not sure I'd believe the answer. Gods are every bit as petty as we are, and Kunama's got a grudge against the others I've never heard a good explanation for."

"You want me to go into that tree, too?" The peace of the

mountains still reigned in her heart, but flames of anger reignited.

"Of course I do. The only two who don't are Kunama and your father."

The older woman laughed at that. "Probably the only thing those two would ever agree on."

"Dad doesn't want me to go into the tree? He's got an odd way of showing it, dragging me all the way out here."

Gossa's mirth faded. "You're no fool, girl, so don't act one. You know why you're here, and if you let go of your anger for a bit, you'll understand how little Kalen wants you here."

"He lied!" Sascha shouted. Her words echoed off the nearby stones.

Gossa waited, then said. "Sure, he did, and he's paying a hefty price for his lies. That's his problem. Yours is that you can't look past his lies to the truth in front of your face."

Coming from Gossa, the words stung. Sascha bowed her head. "What truth?"

"One that's best found on your own. Like I heard Kalen tell you, there's knowledge and there's knowing, and you need the latter now."

"I'm tiring of vague advice."

"And Kalen is probably tired of you needing everything explained. The best things in life need to be discovered. They can't be given to you."

Sascha sighed. "Fine. What do you want me to do? Walk into that tree with a smile and a wave?"

"I've already told you that's what I want you to do. But what you *need* to do is make a choice. The same one I told you about before. If you can't shoulder this burden, then yes, you may as well claim your own life and give Kalen a chance to live."

Sascha's eyes narrowed. "What did you say?"

Gossa reached into her pocket and pulled out her pouch of runes. She opened it and searched through it until she found the one she was looking for. She held it out for Sascha to examine. "When I cast for you, this was one of the runes that appeared, right beside the rune for parent, or ancestor."

"So?"

"This rune can mean many things. Its root meaning is 'break,' but most often refers to death. The relation to the other runes was clear, and it hinges on your choice. If you choose life and go into that tree, your father will die. But if you choose to end your own life, he will live, and he will fight the scorpions in your stead."

"The runes told you that?"

"No, girl, just knowing your father is enough. If you die, he'll spend the rest of his life in battle, trying to fill the hole in his heart with blood. The scorpions will be the victims of that rage."

"But if I survive my initiation, he'll die?"

"I believe so."

"And you want me to lead the fight against the scorpions? That's what all this is about. You want the fight."

"I want my clan and family to survive, the same as anyone else."

"Leave me, Gossa." It was the politest she could be. She was no different from Dad.

Gossa debated for a moment, then decided following Sascha's orders was in her best interest. She stood, bowed, and returned to the cave.

Sascha searched for the peace she'd felt before Gossa's arrival, but it was nowhere to be found. Higher up the mountain, she spotted a tall cliff face. She imagined climbing to the top, spreading her arms out wide, and flying. Better a quick end than the slow end the growing power within her promised. She'd watched Mom waste away from illness and wanted none of that for herself.

When she turned back, she noticed she wasn't alone.

"I should kill you," she said.

Vilkas laughed. "So like your father. I'm sure if I were to appear in the cave below, he'd have his hands around my throat before I even greeted him."

"He'd be right to do so. You've ruined our lives."

Vilkas didn't answer the accusation. "Have you decided?"

"No."

Vilkas leaned back and planted his hands behind him, stretching. He wasn't bothered by her glare.

"Why?" she asked.

"To enjoy the view. It's been many years since I've come home. It feels good to be back."

"I don't care why you're here. I want to know why you're doing this."

"If you want that answer, you'll have to survive the initiation."

She punched him right in the cheek. His head snapped to one side, but her fist didn't even wipe the smile from his face.

He rubbed where she'd hit him. "Not even Kalen was bold enough for that."

She stood, but there was nowhere to go. She couldn't outrun a god, and the cave offered no shelter. The feelings inside her built until she felt like she might explode. She screamed until her throat was raw. When she could scream no more, she sobbed, the tears her only release.

"You are so much like him," Vilkas said.

"Stop saying that!" Sascha shouted. "I'm nothing like him!"

"Hasn't he told you? The night before the battle, he came to a high place just like this. He prayed and cried, too. There was less shouting, though."

"Just leave me alone!" she screamed.

Vilkas's smile never faltered. But he stood and traced his finger on the boulder. Where his finger passed, a small mark was etched upon the stone. His finger moved quickly and gracefully. When he finished, he stepped away so she could see it clearly. It had the look of one of Vilkas's runes, but she'd never seen it before.

The sight cooled her temper. "What is it?"

"May I give you a nugget of wisdom before I leave?"

She blew a loose strand of hair out of her face. "Why not? Everyone else has."

"Runes are just runes. It's up to you to decide what to do with them."

She glared at him. "Fine. You've shared your great wisdom. Now, what is it?"

"It's a rune your father never learned. Its root is 'peace.'"

With that, he was gone. If not for the mark on the stone, she would have sworn she'd imagined the brief encounter. But the rune remained. She ran her own finger across it, tracing the same marks Vilkas had made. Her finger was smaller than his, but she felt the unnatural smoothness of the stone where he'd carved the sign.

She sighed and sat back down on the boulder. She looked out on the mountains, focusing on nothing in particular. Her fists unclenched, and she took a deep breath.

It was beautiful here.

She'd always loved the endless fields of Bonde's lands,

but the mountains captured her imagination. This was a land she could explore for the rest of her life and still not understand all its secrets. Somewhere far away, a wolf howled, and Sascha thought it sounded lonely.

She turned her gaze to the cliff, but it lacked the appeal it had before. She didn't want to die. Not really. But she didn't want to enter that tree, either.

The thoughts slowly slipped away, and her mind went blank. She stared off into the distance and let the vista become a part of her. The northern breeze blew through her hair like it did the grass, and when the wolf howled again, it sang to her, sending a shiver down her spine. When the wind was angled just right, she smelled the roasting meat from the cave below.

They were moments, not unlike every other moment she'd lived through. But they were more vivid, penetrating past the normal cloud of thoughts running through her mind and straight to her heart. She shivered again, this time in ecstasy.

In time, the sensations faded. Her thoughts returned, though they were quieter than before, like whispers she could ignore. She couldn't remember deciding, but the decision had been made all the same.

She stood and stretched, a hint of a smile spreading across her face.

Then she walked down to the cave to join the others.

INITIATION

Kalen led the way to Vilkas's tree as the sun fell low in the sky. His feet felt like they were weighted with stones as he trudged up the side of the mountain. Already he glimpsed the top of the tree, its leaves rustling in the breeze. They'd come so far, but now it was too close.

The path was familiar. He'd walked this route dozens of times in his youth, maybe even hundreds. As his clan had withered, more families sent their children to the tree. What had once been a choice for only a brave few became a necessity for the desperate remainder. Some moons, the tree took almost as many souls as war.

The experience had never failed to excite his youthful dreams. Young men and women, who'd once been the older children he'd played with, walked boldly toward their new future. If their steps faltered, or they glanced back to their parents in fear, young Kalen didn't notice. They were his heroes and could do no wrong. He prayed every night that when his turn came, he would approach the tree with the same courage.

His youthful idealism hadn't masked the anguish of the parents, though. Kalen had seen blooded warriors weep and had never understood why. Didn't the parents know their children approached glory?

This night, he remembered how narrow his vision had once been, and he cursed his past self that had judged so harshly. No parent worth the title wanted to see their child suffer.

This night, he took strength from Sascha. She walked calmly behind him, her step lighter than before. Gossa had returned to the cave, reporting that she'd failed to persuade Sascha of anything, but when Sascha had returned after, the change was noticed by all.

Perhaps it wasn't fair to her, but Kalen thought that for the first time, Sascha carried herself as a woman grown. True, she'd mostly been caring for herself for years now, but the way she walked was more mature than before. She looked more like Embla than ever. His heart ached at the thought.

Sascha had said little in the cave, and there'd been a stillness surrounding her. She ate and slept, then rested some more. Once more, she left the cave, asking that no one follow her. She had returned in time to eat again and follow him toward the tree.

Only the two of them walked this last part of the journey. Kalen had asked Gossa and the other foxes to remain behind. The Initiation of Vilkas was supposed to be a mystery to outsiders, and though the prohibition seemed foolish now that the wolves were as good as gone, it seemed right to uphold the traditions to the end. He was glad that it was just the two of them here at the end of their quest. He kept his raging emotions deep within as he endeavored to imitate her peaceful walk.

His throat ached as they grew closer to the tree. His own initiation had haunted his dreams for almost a year after, but there was no denying the success of the ritual. Only after his initiation had he learned the skills necessary to create Fang. He remembered branches of the tree wrapping around his throat, choking the life from him as he struggled helplessly. He'd been unable to draw a breath but also unable to die. Swords had cut at him, hacked off limbs that reappeared one tortured, choked-off scream later.

What kind of monster was he to put his precious daughter through the same?

Each step toward the tree brought forth a long-buried memory of Sascha's childhood. She was an infant, grabbing onto his finger with her tiny hands, squeezing with more strength than he thought was possible. He'd been so afraid in those early days to hold her, worried he would somehow break her in his massive hands. She was a child grinning widely when she first put an arrow through a target. She was a girl crying as they returned Embla to Bonde's embrace.

Then she was beside him, and they looked upon Vilkas's tree together. He'd forgotten how big it was. The tree was an ash tree, though several times larger than any other. It stretched both high and wide, casting enough shade to protect a small village from the summer sun. The tree was surrounded by a circle of stone, Vilkas's runes carefully etched on each of the markers. Kalen reached out to touch a low-hanging leaf, the air so thick with energy he could nearly grasp it. Vilkas might be diminished, but incredible power remained in this place.

After a brief pause, Sascha stepped toward the tree, and Kalen's stomach dropped. They needed more time.

"Sascha," he said.

She stopped and turned, but he had nothing to say. He wanted to reach out and embrace her, but feared she would reject any attempt. "I love you."

She swallowed and nodded, then turned back to the tree.

His knees shook, and he almost fell, but he fought the weakness. If she looked back, he wanted her to see him standing tall, proud of her.

Watching her walk toward the tree was as hard as watching Embla waste away. He believed in her. If anyone could survive Vilkas's trials, it was his daughter. But even assuming she survived, the Sascha that emerged from the tree would be someone new. In a way, this would be the last time he saw his little girl.

A knot in the tree swirled and grew wider, then expanded into a crack that opened into a passage. The inside of the tree was dark, but Sascha didn't hesitate. She walked straight in without a glance back.

The tree closed around her, and it was a giant ash once again.

Kalen took a deep breath. He fought a losing battle against the emotions raging in his chest.

It wasn't long before her screams began.

Kalen sat, watching the land he'd once called home. Sometimes he paced. Near the ring of stones, he found a heavy stick perfect for sword practice. He trained his cuts until his arms, back, and shoulders burned.

Even that did little to distract him from Sascha's suffering. Her screams were regular companions, waking him both day and night. They sounded hollow and far away, and he was grateful they rarely lasted long. Long periods of silence were worse, though. Silence did nothing to limit his imagination, and he feared Sascha hadn't been strong enough. But the tree never opened to disgorge her lifeless body, and in time, she would scream again.

The days were long and his watch difficult, but whenever he felt pity for his position, he reminded himself of the trials Sascha suffered.

Gossa occasionally visited to deliver food and water, and to check on Kalen. She never remained long. The foxes were busy as Jolon neared. The great scorpion commander had pushed his horses past the breaking point, and they were now on foot. Gossa's foxes kept a quiet watch on the advance, reporting to Gossa using means Kalen couldn't guess. The advance layered one more worry on top of Kalen's already considerable burden. It looked like Sascha would finish her trial before Jolon's arrival, but it would be close, and any delay might prove fatal.

The worst of it was that there was nothing to do but watch and wait.

Kalen prayed to Vilkas, just as he had when he was younger, but the old man was nowhere to be found. He'd expected Vilkas to visit soon after they returned to familiar territory, but the god was silent, just as he always was when Kalen needed him most.

Kalen stood guard beside the tree for two nights and three days, watching and worrying. The third night was supposed to be the last. By the time the sun rose again, the tree would open, and Sascha would emerge, reborn with the full strength of Vilkas. Kalen imagined the scene hundreds of times as he waited.

As dusk fell on the third night, Gossa appeared once more. The look on her face told Kalen the news was bad before she spoke. "How long until Sascha completes the trial?" she asked.

They'd spoken of this several times before, but Kalen repeated the same answer without judgment. Gossa wore her concern like a weighted cloak that slowed her otherwise quick steps. "Usually somewhere near the middle of the night tonight."

Gossa swore. "Vilkas is a damn fool for creating such a long trial."

Kalen kept his peace. "Jolon is close?"

"If we leave him unopposed, he will be at the tree before Sascha emerges. He has pushed harder than I thought possible. Is there any way of speeding the trial?"

"If there were, I would have taken it long before."

Gossa continued to search for hope, when only one solution remained. "Is there any chance of her emerging early?" she asked.

"A slim one, but not one we can depend on. If he will reach the tree so soon, our only option is to fight him before he reaches it."

Gossa glared at Kalen for a moment, then grew more thoughtful. "We've avoided direct conflict with the scorpions for a reason, Kalen. While uncertainty remains regarding Sascha's success, I'd be a fool to send my warriors into battle."

Kalen tapped the hilt of Fang. Any other option would have been better, but this moment felt as though it had been fated for a very long time. He breathed out his last frustrations. It was time to stop running. "You won't lose. I'll join the assault if you attack, but I can't defeat the scorpions alone."

Gossa considered. "My runes claimed that if Sascha stepped into that tree, you would likely die. Now I understand why."

Kalen shrugged. "If it will be, it will be, but don't put too much faith in runes. Should that future come to pass, though, I'd ask you to watch after her and help her as best you can."

Gossa bit her lower lip. She stared at the tree, then decided. "The foxes you've met aren't the only ones in the area. Our clan is weaker than the wolves were when they were wiped out, but we'll spend the last of our strength to aid you and Sascha."

Kalen bowed. "Thank you. I promise you we will win this battle, no matter the cost."

JOLON

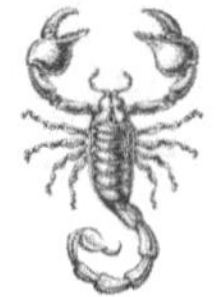

Jolon swore as one of his trusted commanders took an arrow through the chest. He should have completed the destruction of the damned foxes years ago, but they were so diminished he hadn't been concerned. He should have known better. There was nothing more dangerous than a wounded animal with no escape. His own life was proof enough of that.

The foxes skilled enough to survive this long were the toughest that remained. Years of Jolon's expansion had killed the weak, leaving only the best. For that, Jolon figured the foxes owed him a debt of gratitude, though he wouldn't waste his breath seeking it. Maybe, if he had the chance to choke the life out of Gossa, he would demand her thanks before she died.

Not that many warriors opposed him, but they fought like a force with many times their number. They scurried in and out of cracks, appearing like ghosts with their short bows in hand. They would launch a shaft or three, then disappear back into the mountain as though he had imagined them.

The haste he'd demanded rushing up here had already weakened Jolon's forces. Only forty or so had survived the trek into Vilkas's land, and the number was now half that thanks to the damned archers. Wisdom and caution dictated a retreat, but that wasn't an option. Kunama screamed in the back of his mind, afraid of the girl stuck in the tree. Combined with Jolon's fear of Kalen, only one path to victory remained.

Both needed to die tonight.

No one had spotted Kalen yet, but Jolon knew the bastard was nearby. He waited for the foxes to soften up Jolon's warriors, and then he'd strike, ripping through them with his cursed sword.

If Jolon lost many more of his best, he'd be in no position to deliver the justice Kalen deserved. He hadn't wanted to reveal his power before Kalen appeared, but if he didn't, he'd have to fight the foxes alone.

An arrow came for his head, but his sharpened senses warned him. He tilted his head to the left, and the arrow sliced through the air where his skull had been. The archer was up on the mountainside, confident none of the scorpions could reach him before he crawled back into his hole. It was time to prove him wrong.

He called upon Kunama and felt fresh strength wash over him. He sprinted up the side of the mountain, putting the goats who called this land home to shame. Every step launched him higher. He took delight in the wide eyes of the fox, who had thought he was safe just a moment before.

Jolon whipped his blade from its sheath.

The fox was fast. He leaned back, and Jolon almost

missed. The tip of Jolon's sword did nothing but slice into the knuckle of the hand holding the bow. The archer reached for his blade, but before his hand could grasp the hilt, a spasm wracked his body.

The archer's stamina was pathetic. A true warrior should have been able to endure the scorpion's sting long enough to finish the fight and die with honor. This weak fox lacked the strength to even draw his sword. Jolon spit on him and looked around.

He ducked as another arrow sought his life. This one had been aimed at his chest. Another fox had appeared farther up the mountain. She turned to hide, but he reached her as she slipped back into her burrow. He stabbed out with his dagger, and she froze in the entrance, blocking any other archers planning on using the same passage.

His presence shifted the course of the battle. A few more archers emerged as they marched toward the tree, but most had learned their lesson. Jolon suspected they would gather now and make one last defensive stand.

That was where he would find Kalen.

The remaining scorpions stuck close together, senses sharp. Less than twenty remained, but it would be enough. Some of his best warriors fought by his side, and they would buy him the time to duel with Kalen and finish the fight that had started when he was a child.

Memories of that night still haunted him. He'd been a child who was just learning the ways of Kunama. His weak sword skills disappointed Father, but his lack of skill with the sword was overlooked for his incredible aptitude with Kunama's runes. That night he'd trained with Father personally, practicing with the wooden sword one of the other warriors had carved for him.

Despite being Father's son, Jolon didn't remember his life being any easier than the other children's. If anything, Father worked him harder than anyone else. Jolon had welcomed the challenge, knowing how difficult it would be to someday fill Father's role.

He and Father had finished their training and were enjoying a very late supper when Kalen struck. Most of the other scorpions were already asleep, and afterward, Jolon learned Kalen had killed many while they slumbered. By the time the scorpions understood the danger, it was too late. Fang glowed with Vilkas's runes, shining through the blood that coated it from crossguard to tip.

Jolon had watched Father fight, certain the crime would end with their duel. No scorpion could fight Father and win, and Jolon hadn't been able to follow the swords as they clashed under a moonless night. But it had ended with Father on his knees, calmly trying to scoop his organs back into his stomach and invoke Kunama's healing runes.

Kalen had taken Father's head while he held no weapon.

Father's death marked Jolon's greatest loss, but the moments after marked his greatest shame. Instead of taking up Father's sword and seeking revenge, Jolon cast unsight over himself. He curled into the corner of a tent while Kalen savagely murdered the rest of his clan. He cupped his hands over his head while Kunama's greatest warriors fought to the death, and didn't emerge until dawn.

He found Father's body, the head taken as proof of Kalen's great deed.

There were survivors, but not many. From that day forward, the suffering and hardship Jolon had known increased tenfold. He had to learn all that his father didn't have time to teach him, all while keeping the last of the clan intact. Only his close relationship with Kunama allowed him to push forward. Bit by bit, he'd struggled to where he stood today.

Today, Kalen paid for his sins. When that was done, Jolon would turn his attention south and make Bonde's chiefs pay for unleashing Kalen upon the scorpions. Justice was long in coming, but it was here.

They turned the corner of the path. Around the next bend, the top of Vilkas's tree could be seen above the ridge.

The scorpions walked into a flight of arrows, and a large man drew a sword with a glow Jolon had never forgotten.

Kalen was here to meet his doom.

TRIAL

Sascha thought that she had understood suffering. She'd watched Mom waste away before her eyes, unable to change a thing. Mom's death broke their family apart, severing the ties that Sascha had taken for granted. She and Dad shared a house and split many of the chores, but Sascha woke every morning feeling alone and went to sleep feeling forgotten.

Vilkas quickly taught her how little she knew. Thousands of needles poked her skin as each of her fingers was broken. She'd thought the bruises and cuts she'd suffered throughout her childhood were as bad as pain could be, but she soon learned the different flavors of hurt, from the dull ache of a body that refused to move to the piercing agony of a spear through her side.

She screamed and wept at the pain, and in the blink of an eye, it vanished. Her body floated in an infinite void, and when she held her hands to her face, they looked unharmed. Though she could see her hands and body easily, there was no source of light.

Time had no meaning, and boredom soon took hold. She twisted and swam, but there was no change in her situation. She cried for what felt like a long time. When her tears dried, she screamed for help until her throat was raw. Nothing changed. She floated in the void, helpless like a child.

Her thoughts wandered until there was nothing more to think, and then her mind went quiet. That was when she noticed the void wasn't exactly what she had thought it was. It wasn't empty. The vibrations and pulses were subtle, nothing more than the slightest flutter of a butterfly's wings.

Instinctively, she connected to Vilkas's rune of awareness. The void took on shape and form, and before long, she was standing outside the tree. At first, she thought the trials were over, but the world was too vivid, and she couldn't feel the brush of air on her skin.

She spun slowly around and saw Vilkas sitting beside the tree, that same smile on his face. "You found me. Congratulations on completing your first trial."

Though he had caused so much pain, she didn't feel any urge to attack him. That confused her, and the question leaped from her lips. "Why am I not angry with you?"

His smile grew wider, revealing sharpened teeth. "No one asks that question first. They all complain about the suffering it takes to get here. I'm impressed. In answer to your question, you've moved beyond your emotions, at least for a bit. If your focus wavers for too long, your anger will return, and you will return to the void."

"What happens next?"

"You'll find out soon enough. This is a place to rest between the trials. As a reward, and as encouragement, you've earned yourself the answer to any single question. I'll answer truthfully."

"What do you want from me? What do you think all of this will accomplish?"

Vilkas held up two fingers. "That's two questions, but I'll forgive you, as one answer suffices. I suppose you could say I'm acting out of selfish interest. I'm fading, Sascha. Kalen is now the last pure wolf, and the time of his service to me draws to a close. I will not die, but I will become something else, and the power of my runes will fade. My fate is inevitable now. But I want something of myself to live on. I think my ideas still have value. I want you to go out into the world and spread the best of my teachings."

Sascha wasn't sure what to make of that, but Vilkas gave her little time to consider.

"There's your answer, so you best prepare yourself, for the second trial now begins," he said.

He moved faster than Sascha could follow. She felt herself being picked up and thrown at the tree. A branch wrapped around her neck and pulled her tight to the tree. Her eyes went wide as she tried to breathe and couldn't. She screamed, but her scream was cut off when she saw Vilkas with a spear in his hand. He pierced her in the side and pinned her to the tree. She screamed again, but the branches tightened around her neck and cut her off.

"Free yourself," Vilkas said, and he vanished.

Sascha grabbed at the branch and pulled, but her strength was meaningless. She called upon Vilkas's runes, strengthening her limbs, but to no avail. She wiggled and squirmed, but the embedded spear sent waves of agony up her spine, exploding in her skull.

When she gasped for air, all she felt was the barest tickle

down her throat. She wrapped her hands around the spear and pulled, earning only another wave of pain for her efforts.

As in the void, she cried and screamed. She cursed Vilkas for his selfishness, and she cursed Dad for every sin she could think of. She was supposed to be in the village, kissing Rolf and dreaming of a day when they made their own lives, not hanging from a tree with a spear in her side.

The sun went down, and the moon chased it across the sky. The sun rose behind Sascha, and the cycle repeated. Agony and exhaustion blended with hunger and thirst. Her tongue was dry and swollen and stuck to the roof of her mouth. The sun went down again, and she despaired.

By the time the sun rose again, she'd surrendered. She couldn't breathe, but death refused to take her and end her suffering. Her blood dripped from the end of the spear, forming a pool that the roots of the tree sipped hungrily. She was going to die here in this meaningless world Vilkas had created. Once again, her mind was quiet.

It wasn't real.

A person couldn't choke and bleed out for three days. Though her hunger and thirst seemed real, she still had never felt a breeze on her skin nor the warmth of the sun as it set and shone on her.

She closed her eyes and imagined the tree letting go and the spear disappearing. At the beginning of the trial, such focus wouldn't have been possible. The pain was too consuming. Now, though, it was a simple matter. She connected the dream to her will, and she was free. She breathed deeply, only to realize there was still no air. There never had been.

All illusion.

She thought of a full waterskin, and one appeared in her hand. She took a sip and decided that water had never tasted better.

Vilkas appeared beside her. "Impressive."

Once again, she felt none of the anger she felt was justified. She took another sip and smiled, her expression matching Vilkas's. She seemed lighter, as though she could run across the top of a cloud without a problem. "You're stripping away the layers of my illusions."

Vilkas nodded. "Clever, too. It's fitting that the last of these is one of the most interesting trials I've ever done."

"Is it hard for you, torturing your wolves like this?"

"Unbearably so. Most gods refuse to push as hard as I do. But none master runes like my children master mine."

"That's what all this is about?"

"The runes connect you to fundamental forces, powers even more primal than me and my brethren. To use them best, one needs to be as close to the truth as possible, and that's a painful process. Horrible as this is, it's the fastest and most successful way I've found."

"What good does any of this do in the real world?"

"Do you think the real world is any less an illusion than this one?" Vilkas asked.

The question shook Sascha to her core, and she didn't have an answer.

"Are you prepared for the final trials?" he asked.

"Don't I get a question?"

"You've been asking them since you freed yourself from the tree. But there's no need. The question you want to ask most will be answered in the next trial."

"What's next? Constant drowning, or being lit on fire?"

"You must face the most difficult illusion of all. Those of your own creation. The lies that define your entire life."

"It's Dad who lies, not me."

"Partially true."

"What do I lie about?"

"When you were on that tree, where did you think you belonged?"

"Back home."

Vilkas's smile faded. "That village in Bonde's land was never your home. It is the first and greatest lie, and one you still believe in your bones."

"I've lived my whole life there!"

"And you were never supposed to."

Sascha squeezed her eyes shut, trying to understand. "What do you mean? You were the one who ordered my dad to escape to Bonde's land."

Vilkas grunted. "No, I didn't."

Sascha took a step back, and her world collapsed around her. She'd never imagined that everything she believed could be so fragile, but the last few moons had battered her sense of self until almost nothing remained. She clung desperately to the idea that Dad had stolen her from the place where she belonged, that none of this was supposed to have happened.

"What do you mean?"

Vilkas waved a hand. "Let me show you."

The tree disappeared, and they were on another mountain peak near the middle of the night. Below, Sascha could see two camps separated by a ridge. One was much larger than the other. Then she saw Dad. He was much younger and less careworn, but it was unmistakably him. He was on hands and knees, praying and crying.

She'd never seen him so, not even on the day Mom died. It twisted her stomach to see Dad on his knees.

The stars raced across the sky, but Dad remained alone.

"You never visited him that night," Sascha said.

"Let me show you what was supposed to happen," Vilkas said.

Night turned to day, and Dad led the wolves in a battle that put their ambush of the scorpions to shame. Fang spilled enough blood to fill a lake, and the surviving chiefs of the opposing clans bent their knees. Dad became the chief of all clans, and Sascha became living proof that the lines between the clans were blurring. Dad led the clans to a time of peace, growing numerous and spreading from mountain to plain. When he died in his sleep, Sascha became chief in his stead, and the expansion continued.

The scene died, and they were once again before the tree. Vilkas grunted. "Instead, the wolves died that day, and now the scorpions seek to conquer and destroy. Many clans are on the verge of sharing the fate of the wolves. Kalen had one last trial, but he became a coward and ran, all because of you and Embla."

"Why didn't you just tell him?" The storm of emotions within Sascha rumbled in her stomach. "If you just spoke clearly, there'd be no problems! He was desperate for your guidance."

"For the same reason I can't simply appear and tell you the world is an illusion. It's the truth you've suffered days for. But you've heard this before: there's knowledge and then there's knowing. The same was true of your father. He needed to make the choice to fight, knowing it would be one of the hardest in his life, so that he would develop the courage to make the hard choices that would lead to the peace you witnessed. If I'd told him, then he wouldn't be a leader. He'd only be following my commands, and he'd fail later."

Sascha growled. She kept returning to the scenes of her as a chief, longing for them. Dad had stolen that from her because he was a coward. She screamed again, causing the illusion to waver and temporarily fade to black. She stopped before she'd gone too far, and then the tears came.

It all seemed so enormously unfair. "Gods, I hate him!"

Vilkas smiled, as if he'd been waiting for exactly that proclamation. "Let me show you everything else he hasn't told you about."

Scenes flashed, and she saw Dad as Vilkas saw him, understanding every action he took. Mom and Dad fled from the mountains and across the plains. Dad, begging entrance into Bonde's lands and arguing with the chiefs about the cost. Finally, head hung low, he agreed to attack Kunama, setting in motion events that echoed to this very day.

She watched Dad slaughter the sleeping scorpions, then saw him collapse in tears as he fled the scene.

Months passed in heartbeats, and Dad was a shell of the man he'd once been. He threw himself into the building of the house, learning how from some farmers. She watched him eagerly hide Fang under the floorboards, desperate to put his past behind him.

Sascha saw Mom's worry, even as her belly grew. There was no fire in Dad's eyes, and he sometimes went the whole day without moving much.

The spark didn't return until Sascha was born. It was a dim flicker of life, but in time, he returned to being the man she knew. She watched him clean and feed her. He held her to his chest and sang to her as she slept.

Sascha's throat tightened at the joy and affection she witnessed on Dad's face.

It was hard to believe he had once looked at her like that.

The scenes continued, one after the other. Dad, hunting so that she would have fresh meat to eat. Dad, working in the field to bring in a share of the harvest for the family. Small moments, none that had mattered at the time. They quickly reached times she remembered. Dad, pressing a cool cloth against Mom's forehead. Dad, crying alone in his bed the day after she died. Then he was standing outside her closed door, listening to her sobbing with anguish on his face. And finally, Dad cooking breakfast and telling her they had to leave.

Taken together, the scenes told a truth that was unavoidable.

Vilkas waved a hand, and a feast appeared before her. "If you can find your center now, the third trial is halfway over. You should best be quick, for our time grows short." He vanished again.

She sniffed and wiped the snot from her nose. If he'd left food, she might as well eat it. She suspected Vilkas did nothing without reason. The meal was among the best she'd ever eaten, and the act of filling her belly calmed the thoughts that crashed in her head.

Once she was full, she lay back in the grass beside the tree and stared up into its leaves. She was tired with exhaustion that settled deep in her bones, but her thoughts prevented sleep. Her memories of Dad conflicted with the scenes Vilkas had shown her. She didn't think Vilkas had shown her anything false, but she couldn't forget all her anger.

Sasha did not know how long she lay under the tree. The

sun had stopped moving in the sky, trapping her in perpetual day.

Finally, she let go.

It was too tiring carrying everything, like she'd hiked all day with a loaded pack. It was far easier to wrap up all her stories and all her beliefs and just leave them by the side of the road, relics of her past.

Her breath came easily, and the sun crawled across the sky once again.

When she sat up, Vilkas was in front of her.

He handed her a knife. "One last trial. If you pass, you leave, and just in time." He waved his hand, and they were still sitting by the tree, but now she saw a battle taking place in the distance.

"Kalen fights one last time," Vilkas said.

The fight faded, and they were once again alone.

"And if I fail?" Sascha asked.

"You'll return to the void."

Sascha held the knife up. "What am I supposed to do with this?"

"There's only one last understanding you need to embrace. That your life is meaningless. If you wish to win your life back, first you must lose it."

Sascha stared at the knife. The edge was as sharp as anything she'd ever seen. Of all the trials, this one seemed the easiest to pass. Her life was meaningless. Once, Vilkas had planned a glorious future for her, but Dad's moment of cowardice had taken that from her. The realization didn't make her want to scream or shout. She accepted what had happened and accepted the consequence.

Sascha turned the knife toward her, positioning the tip in a place and at an angle where it would pierce her heart. She watched Vilkas for any sign he was proud, but his face was a mask.

She hesitated. It was one thing to claim her life was meaningless, and she understood everything around her was an illusion, but it was still difficult to summon the courage.

It would be like flying, she decided.

She gripped the handle with both hands and pulled. The knife slid into her chest. It hurt, but after the last few days, it barely seemed like anything at all. She looked at Vilkas. The old god's smile had faded.

"Oh, Sascha," he said, and there was so much pity and sympathy in his voice that his words brought tears to her eyes.

Before she could ask anything, she fell back, and the world went dark.

When she came to, she was floating once again in an endless void.

FANG'S LAST BLOOD

Gossa's foxes had been more successful than Kalen had dared hope. Less than twenty of Kunama's warriors entered the small pass where they'd set their final ambush. Every scorpion had their sword drawn. They charged at Kalen, kicking up dirt and loose stone as they ran.

Kalen's attention fell on one warrior who stood near the center of the press. Little about his appearance was concerning. His clothes were as worn and dirty as anyone else's. He stood a full head shorter than any of the other warriors. But the aura emanating from him made his identity clear.

Jolon had arrived to finish the battle.

Drawing Fang was an easier choice than it had been against Naga. He saw no actual choice. This fight had been written upon his fate, maybe from the night he had fled the wolves' last battle. Fang jumped from its sheath and Kalen met the charge. To both sides of him, arrows cut through the air, finding the hearts of Kunama's warriors.

Kalen drew upon Vilkas's runes. This close to the tree,

they were stronger than Kalen had felt in years. Combined with the power contained within Fang, the scorpions had no chance.

He fell upon his enemies with a fury. Fang left a trail of runic light and blood as it cut into the heart of the scorpion advance. One scorpion stabbed at him, but Fang deflected the sword, nearly skewering a scorpion seeking to attack Kalen from behind. The stabbing scorpion reacted quickly, withdrawing his sword so as not to strike an ally, but the moment of reaction gave Kalen all the time he needed to cut through the man's neck.

Most of the scorpions had runes etched along their thin blades. They were likely skilled warriors in their own right. But none of the swords were Fang, and none of the warriors were Kalen. They fought better than the young hunters Naga had traveled with, but they couldn't match Kalen's strength or experience.

Gossa's archers menaced the fight as well. If the scorpions turned too much attention on Kalen, they died with arrows in their backs.

Jolon realized the same after almost half his remaining forces were wiped out in Kalen's initial assault. He shouted in their language, and the scorpions turned away from Kalen to focus their attention on the archers. Kalen turned to punish them for ignoring him, but Jolon's attack prevented him from following through.

Jolon's blade flickered in the last light of the moon faster than a snake's tongue. Kalen retreated while he took a measure of the man's strength and technique.

Jolon impressed him quickly. Kalen had expected that the man who'd risen to unite the scorpions and take back all the land they'd lost would be strong, and he wasn't wrong.

The scorpion chief's blade was as fast as Fang, and Kalen noted the slight discoloration along the edge.

Of course, the scorpion would rely on poison.

Kalen parried the next set of cuts, only to be surprised when Jolon's blade snuck through his defense. He leaned back before the blade could cut across his chest.

Jolon pressed the attack, but Kalen had a better sense of his speed now, and Jolon couldn't close the distance without risking his blade and his life. After a few attempts, Jolon broke off and retreated a few paces. Kalen didn't give chase.

Behind them, the sun was just beginning to rise, but he had sensed nothing from Vilkas's tree. Where was Sascha? She should have completed her trial by now. No one had ever emerged alive once the sun rose on the fourth day. But she couldn't fail. Not his girl. He didn't dare glance back, though. One moment of distraction was all Jolon would need to end the fight.

"I don't know why I once feared you," Jolon said in the common tongue. His sword flashed in a complex pattern. "You are old and weak, and your legend will die today."

Kalen summoned Vilkas's strength again.

He blinked, and it was as if Jolon had vanished. He caught movement out of the corner of his eye and turned. Fang deflected the first attack before Kalen was even aware of the danger. Jolon struck and struck again, his steel impossibly fast. Fang kept Kalen safe, and when Jolon got too close, Fang almost took off his head.

Jolon danced back, breathing hard. Kalen cursed to himself. He'd almost killed the chief and ended this. He saw the weakness in Jolon's technique now. The Kunama chief preferred to keep everyone at a distance, where the speed of his blade and the venom along the edge gave him an advantage. But when an enemy got close, he panicked.

There was no panic in his eyes now, though. A wide smile was on his face. He pointed with his sword at Kalen's arm.

Kalen looked down and saw a scratch, so shallow he hadn't even noticed when it had happened.

"This battle is already over," Jolon said. "The scorpion's sting is already running through your blood. The more you fight, the faster it will spread. But even if you were to lie down and recite Vilkas's healing runes, it wouldn't be enough. The gods themselves would die if I stabbed them with this sword. Truthfully, I'm surprised you're still standing."

Kalen wasn't. Fang had healing runes inscribed upon it, a detail few realized. It helped heal him even as it drained the blood from its victims.

Still, now that he'd noticed the scratch, he felt the difference in his body. His blood burned, and his temple throbbed with every beat of his heart. He didn't have long.

One technique remained. A layering of Vilkas's runes that gave him more strength and speed. He'd only used it twice before and regretted it both times. There was a limit to what the runes could do, a way of the world not even the gods challenged. This technique pushed that limit, and his body paid the price. As a young man, both times he'd used the technique had cost him days of recovery.

But he would not survive this battle. He felt the poison rushing through his body. All that remained was to kill Jolon to protect Sascha. He risked a glance back, confident Jolon would bask in the moment of his victory. The sun was just rising over the peaks, and the tree was silent and closed.

Jolon sneered. "Don't worry. Your daughter will be next."

Kalen ignored the scorpion and whispered toward the tree. "Love you, girl."

Then he turned his attention back to Jolon. He tightened his grip on Fang. One last duel, and they could both rest. He whispered the runes, layering abilities on top of one another. His muscles expanded, and his heart beat faster, spreading the poison through his body. He ignored the fiery pain and focused his attention on Jolon.

Kalen attacked, and Jolon's eyes went wide.

Steel clashed, and Kalen was close. Jolon's blade cut lines across Kalen's body, but he was already as good as dead, and the wounds didn't slow his assault. Fang was a blur, cutting into Jolon whenever the scorpion's steel wasn't fast enough to protect him.

Kalen's heart thudded once, then skipped a beat. He coughed up blood and felt his body weaken.

It was too soon. He tried to raise Fang, but the sword felt like a boulder in his hands. He called for Vilkas, but he'd bent the rules of the world too far. The runes wouldn't answer. He slammed his forehead against Jolon's nose as he fell, hoping to drive some fragment of the nose into the monster's brain. Jolon's nose collapsed with a satisfying crunch, but it wasn't fatal, and Kalen fell to his knees. Fang remained in his hand, but he dug the point in the ground and held it tight just to remain upright.

Jolon was a mess. Blood poured over his lips and chin, and his left arm hung limp at his side, almost severed. The bone that Kalen thought was a rib was exposed on Jolon's left side, but Fang hadn't quite cut deep enough.

If he'd been younger, or not poisoned, he thought he

would have succeeded. But he'd been neither, and Jolon still stood.

The scorpion stumbled toward Kalen and poked him with his sword. The tip went into Kalen's chest, right above his heart. Kalen could do nothing but watch. He couldn't even feel the sword with all the other pain competing for his attention.

Jolon stood there, then shook his head. "No. You'll be dead soon enough. You might as well watch the end of everything you loved, just like you made me watch the destruction of my family so long ago."

He pulled the sword out and started walking toward the tree. The archers and scorpions still fought, the battle even for the moment.

Kalen summoned the last of his strength, meaning to turn and attack. None of his wounds were serious. It was only the poison holding him back. But it sapped the strength from his limbs. He could turn, but he couldn't rise from his knees. All his efforts rewarded him with was a view of the end.

Jolon laughed at his struggles, then turned his attention to the tree.

Kalen fought to rise again and failed again. He was forced to watch Jolon step toward the tree, poisoned sword in hand, as darkness closed in around the edges of his vision.

DEATH

Sascha floated in the void and wept. After everything, she had failed the trials. But why? She'd done just as Vilkas had asked. She'd given her life to him, the same way Dad had given everything to him.

And that old monster had sent her back to the void.

She screamed at the unfairness of it all, at the suffering she'd been forced to endure. She screamed until her throat was hoarse, then screamed some more. The void swallowed her screams and offered nothing in return.

When the last of her screams faded, she realized the void wasn't as silent as it had been before. She heard swords clashing and people shouting.

What was happening?

She closed her eyes and sought her center, calling upon Vilkas's runes to expand her awareness.

A battle happened on the path leading to the tree. Gossa's archers fought against another group of people Sascha didn't recognize. Farther away, Dad dueled a short man with the most terrifying aura she'd ever sensed. They were both too fast for Sascha to follow, but when they split apart, Dad looked weakened, and the other man, who had to be Jolon, smiled viciously.

Dad didn't look hurt, but she sensed his aura dimming. Jolon had done something to him.

She heard Jolon threaten her life.

And Dad turned and looked at her, the barest hint of a smile tugging up one corner of his lips. "I love you, girl."

The words echoed in the void and shook her to her core. He knew he was going to die. Gossa's casting was coming true, right before her eyes.

Dad and Jolon fought again, faster than before. It was impossible for any human to move so fast, but they both did. When it was over, Jolon was seriously wounded, but Dad was on his knees.

The scene faded, and Sascha was once again alone in the void.

All the moments Vilkas had shown her returned to mind as Dad's last words continued to echo in the void.

She snarled and found her center. She achieved Vilkas's awareness in a moment, and the void faded. Again, she stood beside the tree. The same battle raged, and it looked like no time at all had passed.

Vilkas's tree wrapped its limbs around her neck and squeezed, but she still had her center and dismissed the illusion. Then she was on the ground in front of the tree. Vilkas sat beside her and offered her a knife. The scene was exactly as it was before. She took the knife and held it in her hand.

"There's only one last understanding you need to embrace. That your life is meaningless. If you wish to win your life back, first you must lose it," Vilkas said.

Dad's last words still echoed in her memories, and she shook her head. She flipped the knife and caught the blade between her thumb and forefinger. She offered it back to Vilkas. "My life isn't meaningless."

She gestured toward the battlefield. The warriors moved slowly, each sword stroke taking enough time Sascha could have finished a skin of water. Dad was on his knees, turning with agonizing slowness toward Sascha. She pointed at him.

"He taught me that. Took me a while to learn, though," she said.

Vilkas's smile returned. The knife vanished. "An excellent answer."

The old god stood. "You'll need to leave soon, but I have a gift for you."

A bow appeared in his hands, etched with runes. Sascha saw many of the same runes that adorned Fang, and some that didn't. She frowned. "I don't want your weapons."

"Fang is a weapon. Its only purpose is to kill. This is a tool which can be used for any purpose you can imagine."

Sascha arched an eyebrow. "Beyond shooting things with it?"

Vilkas's answering smile was enigmatic. "I carved it with wood from this tree. A reminder of our time together. Oh, and these." He handed her a quiver stuffed full of arrows.

"You act like I won't see you again."

"You might not. I'm not sure what will become of me after today."

Sascha put on the quiver and held the bow. It fit her hand perfectly.

Vilkas bowed deeply. "It's been an honor, Sascha. Now, you best hurry. The battle is almost decided."

Kalen wanted to scream, but his throat was tight.

Jolon took a step and then another. Kalen couldn't move his body. His vision narrowed.

Beyond Jolon, the knot in the tree widened and became a passage. Sascha stepped out of the tree with a new bow in hand. Her eyes blazed, and she stood tall.

The sun broke above the mountain peaks a moment later. The day had dawned.

Sascha nocked an arrow with practiced ease and took aim.

Sascha wished Vilkas had given her more time in the tree. Everyone moved so fast out here that there was no time to think.

She breathed out her fear as she took aim. She didn't want to kill Jolon, even after the destruction he had ordered. If it was possible, she didn't want to kill ever again.

But she was no fool. If she didn't let the arrow fly, he would kill her.

She looked at Dad, wishing he could save her. Even now, she couldn't see a fatal wound. Her awareness focused on his aura, weakening still.

Poison was killing him. She saw the discoloration on Jolon's blade.

Jolon stopped and braced himself, ready to deflect her arrow.

She would show him.

She took aim and whispered, invoking familiar runes. Then she let go.

Jolon's heart leaped as soon as she released the arrow. Her aim was so poor that there was nothing he even had to do. He laughed as the arrow split the air to his side.

Naga had told him she was weak, but he hadn't imagined Kalen's daughter could be so pathetic. He wasn't over forty paces away. Any child among the scorpions could make such a shot.

A moment later, he heard a fleshy *thunk* and turned around. The arrow had struck Kalen in the shoulder.

Jolon couldn't help himself. All these years, he'd lived in so much fear. And yes, Kalen was the best warrior he'd ever crossed swords with. It would take him a full moon to heal, at least. If Kalen had used that last technique first, Jolon might be dead.

But Kalen had fallen, and his own daughter had shot him.

He turned back to Sascha, hands on knees, and laughed until he sounded like one of the pathetic wolves howling desperately at the moon.

Kalen looked down at the arrow in disbelief.

His own daughter had shot him.

He'd been prepared to die, but not like this. Jolon's laughter felt like claws raked across his flesh.

He reached up and pulled the arrow from his shoulder,

then frowned. A moment ago, he hadn't been able to move. He flexed his fingers easily, and the pain faded from his head. His blood stopped boiling.

Fang was still in his hand. His grip was reversed, but that wouldn't matter. He only needed one cut. Jolon's laughter slowly died as he took another step toward Sascha. The scorpion wiped tears of triumph from his cheeks.

Though Kalen wanted to layer the runes like he had before, he didn't dare. Using such power again, so soon, would likely have consequences, and Jolon would sense the attack. He called on Vilkas one last time, then rose to his feet.

Kalen took two quick steps and swung Fang with all his might. The attack was less about technique and more about pure strength.

Kalen wasn't sure what alerted Jolon. But the scorpion raised his sword to block Fang.

Jolon's sword dug deep into Fang, then snapped in half. Fang continued its deadly arc, slicing into Jolon's back at stomach's height. It lodged in his spine. Kalen tried yanking it free, but it was stuck.

No matter.

It was a killing blow.

Jolon raised his arm, still holding the bottom half of his weapon. He flipped the grip in his hand and prepared to stab backward. Kalen roared and flexed his enormous arms. Holding tight to the sword that had served him so well, he lifted Jolon off the ground. Jolon's feet twitched as they left the ground, and the chief screamed.

It only lasted for a moment. Fang snapped in half where Jolon's blade had cut into it, and Jolon collapsed to the ground, blood and viscera pouring out of the gaping wound. Kalen stumbled backward, staring at his broken sword.

Jolon's screams turned the battle in favor of the foxes. Distracted by the death throes of their chief, the final scorpions fell to Gossa's warriors.

Then the battlefield fell quiet, and Sascha was running for him, arms outstretched.

A NEW TRAIL

"You shot me," Dad said.

The words condemned her, but there was a smile on his face. She couldn't remember a time when she had seen him so at ease. He'd shed a heavy burden in that last battle, one that would take her time to understand. She looked forward to the challenge.

They sat alone with the last of their supplies between them. The dried meat was tough, but it tasted like freshly roasted venison to her starving tongue. She'd already finished two skins of water and was well on her way to finishing a third.

"You deserved it," she said, matching his smile.

"True enough." He tore into a piece of meat and chewed until it was tender. "It *was* an inspired shot."

"I didn't want to kill him, and I didn't want you to die."

Dad breathed deeply. "Appreciate that. I didn't want to die either."

The foxes were nearby, nursing their wounds and

burying their dead. They left Sascha and Dad alone. Sascha was grateful for the space. They had plenty to talk about.

"I understand why you did what you did, but I'm still furious. It feels like so much of my life has been based on lies," she said.

Dad nodded. She could see the words cut deeper than Jolon's blade, but he bore the wounds silently.

"I need nothing but truth from you from now on," she said.

"You'll have it," he promised.

"So, what do we do now?"

"Honestly? I hoped you had an idea, or that you learned something in the tree that would guide us."

"I was supposed to be a chief," she said.

Dad looked up sharply. "What?"

"Vilkas told me the truth of that night before the battle. That he never appeared. He showed me a future in which you fought and won and eventually became chief of the wolves. I followed in your footsteps."

Dad stared down at his feet for a long time. "Until that night, I'd always fought, confident in my skills and in my clan. But Embla had just told me about you a fortnight prior. It's no excuse, but that's why. To this day, it's the only time I've run from a fight. I've questioned it a thousand times since then and more, but I can never convince myself staying was the right choice."

"What's done is done. The only question is what we do about it now."

"A question I have as well." Gossa approached. "My warriors and I have spoken, and we would invite you both to join us in our winter camp in the west."

"Why? Won't our presence attract the wrath of the scorpions?"

Gossa snorted. "And what of it? The scorpions have numbers, sure, but their real strength came from Jolon. All winter, they will fight amongst themselves for control of the clan. Not that they won't be dangerous come spring, but they are a danger I don't fear. As to why, it's because I saw you stride onto a battlefield with a bow you've never touched before, take one look, and make the only shot that could have changed the course of the battle. If the blood of Vilkas and Bonde running through your veins wasn't enough, your sharp judgment would be."

Sascha blushed at the attention, and thankfully Gossa turned to Dad. "If you join us, I will ensure our finest smiths help you repair Fang."

Dad nodded slowly and scratched at his chin, then shook his head. "Actually, the half of Fang that's in Jolon can stay there. I'll bury the other half somewhere far away," he said, causing both Sascha and Gossa to stare at him.

"Been thinking about it since the battle. I think my time with Fang is done. Time for me to find a new way to live, something closer to what my daughter expected me to be."

"You're going to be a farmer?" Gossa asked incredulously.

"By the gods, no. I just want to find a different way to fight to protect Sascha. Not through farming, though. I've had enough of that for a lifetime. I appreciate your gracious hospitality, though."

Dad looked at her. "What do you think we should do?"

The question took Sascha aback. "Aren't you going to decide?"

Dad shook his head and offered no further explanation.

Sascha now understood part of why he was as at ease. He planned on sharing the burden of their future with her. She thought, for the first time, about what she wanted. The entire trek north, she'd imagined that if they survived, they would return to Bonde's lands. Now she wasn't so interested. Lysabel's village was a peaceful place, but the world was so much wider. She couldn't return to the existence she'd once known.

Gossa and the foxes had always been generous. They'd given their lives to protect Sascha and Dad. The least she could do was accept their invitation. "We'd be happy to join you," she said.

Sascha looked to Dad, halfway expecting him to disagree, but he smiled. "Seems like a good choice," he said.

They spent the next two days in the area. There were bodies to be buried and supplies to be gathered. Sascha spent quite a bit of the time sitting in front of Vilkas's tree, thinking about the old god. He never appeared to her, no matter the circumstance.

On the day of their departure, Dad found her near the base of the tree. "Any sign of him?"

"None. You?"

"I haven't seen him since I broke the guardian pillar way down south. What are you thinking?"

"I don't think Vilkas wants me to be a wolf the way you were a wolf. I think one of the things I hated thinking all the way up here was that this was to make me like you, and I was so focused on your lies that I wanted nothing to do with that. But the more I remember what he said and did, I don't think he wanted a warrior like you. I think he wanted something different."

Kalen held her hand in his. "May I offer a piece of advice?"

"Sure."

"It doesn't matter what he wanted, and if you start thinking that way, you'll spin yourself around in circles. The gods yank us around, but the only direction that matters is the one you choose."

Sascha nodded. It sounded like good advice.

They met with the rest of the foxes and, with one last look at the enormous ash, turned toward the unknown frontier and left Vilkas's land behind.

THE ADVENTURES CONTINUE!

Top of the morning!

I hope that wherever you are in the world, this finds you doing well. Thanks for reading, and I hope you enjoyed the story. Normally this would be the part of the book where I would tell you about the next installment in the series, but I wrote this book to stand alone.

If you enjoyed this story and would like to check out more of my work, please come visit at RyanKirkauthor.com. There's a serialized novel that's free to read, as well as deals on book bundles you won't find anywhere else.

Once again, in this age of limitless entertainment, I can't thank you enough for spending your time in these pages.

Until next time,

Ryan

April 2023

ALSO BY RYAN KIRK

Saga of the Broken Gods

Band of Broken Gods

Fall of Forgotten Gods

Rise of the Resurrected God

Last Sword in the West

Last Sword in the West

Eyes of the Hidden World

A Sword Named Vengeance

Wraith's Revenge

Frontier's End

Oblivion's Gate

The Gate Beyond Oblivion

The Gates of Memory

The Gate to Redemption

Relentless

Relentless Souls

Heart of Defiance

Their Spirit Unbroken

The Nightblade Series

Nightblade

World's Edge

The Wind and the Void

Blades of the Fallen

Nightblade's Vengeance

Nightblade's Honor

Nightblade's End

Standalone Novels

Blades of Shadow

The Primal Series

Primal Dawn

Primal Darkness

Primal Destiny

ABOUT THE AUTHOR

Ryan Kirk is the bestselling author of the *Nightblade* series of books. When he isn't writing, you can probably find him playing disc golf or hiking through the woods.

www.waterstonemedia.net
contact@waterstonemedia.net

 facebook.com/waterstonemedia
 twitter.com/waterstonebooks
 instagram.com/waterstonebooks